"Running away, again, Dr. Tornell? And yet aren't you the expert at teaching women to stand their ground and face their fears, look reality in the eye?"

"Yes. But I'm also the expert who says women should trust their gut, and my gut says you are dangerous—"

He laughed, and his laughter silenced her.

She lifted her chin. "I'm deadly serious, Sheikh Fehr."

He smiled, but his eyes were cold. "Then act like a scientist, because that's what I want. I'm most certainly not interested in the woman in you."

"That's good, because the woman in me despises the man in you."

Dear Reader,

Harlequin Presents® is all about passion, power and seduction—along with oodles of wealth and abundant glamour. This is the series of the rich and the superrich. Private jets, luxury cars and international settings that range from the wildly exotic to the bright lights of the big city! We want to whisk you away to the far corners of the globe and allow you to escape to and indulge in a unique world of unforgettable men and passionate romances. There is only one Harlequin Presents. And we promise you the world....

As if this weren't enough, there's more! More of what you love every month. Two weeks after the Presents titles hit the shelves, four Presents EXTRA titles go on sale! Presents EXTRA is selected especially for you—your favorite authors and much-loved themes have been handpicked to create exclusive collections for your reading pleasure. Now there are more excuses to indulge! Each month, there's a new collection to treasure—you won't want to miss out.

Harlequin Presents—still the original and the best!

Best wishes,

The Editors

Jane Porter

DUTY, DESIRE AND THE DESERT KING

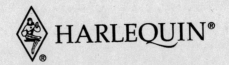

TORONTO • NEW YORK • LONDON
AMSTERDAM • PARIS • SYDNEY • HAMBURG
STOCKHOLM • ATHENS • TOKYO • MILAN • MADRID
PRAGUE • WARSAW • BUDAPEST • AUCKLAND

Recycling programs
for this product may
not exist in your area.

ISBN-13: 978-0-373-23644-2

DUTY, DESIRE AND THE DESERT KING

First North American Publication 2009.

Copyright © 2009 by Jane Porter.

www.eHarlequin.com

Printed in U.S.A.

All about the author...
Jane Porter

Born in Visalia, California, I'm a small-town girl at heart. As a little girl I spent hours on my bed, staring out the window, dreaming of far-off places, fearless knights and happy-ever-after endings. In my imagination I was never the geeky bookworm with the thick Coke-bottle glasses, but a princess, a magical fairy, a Joan-of-Arc crusader.

My parents fed my imagination by taking our family to Europe for a year when I was thirteen. The year away changed me (I wasn't a geek for once!), and overseas I discovered a huge and wonderful world with different cultures and customs. I loved everything about Europe, but felt especially passionate about Italy and those gorgeous Italian men (no wonder my very first Presents hero was Italian).

I confess, after that incredible year in Europe, the travel bug bit, and I spent much of my high school and college years abroad, studying in South Africa, Japan and Ireland.

After my years of traveling and studying I had to settle down and earn a living. With my bachelor's degree from UCLA in American studies, a program that combines American literature and American history, I've worked in sales and marketing, and as a director of a nonprofit foundation. Later I earned my master's in writing from the University of San Francisco and taught junior high and high school English.

I now live in rugged Seattle, Washington, with my two young sons. I never mind a rainy day, either, because that's when I sit at my desk and write stories about faraway places, fascinating people and, most importantly of all, love.

Jane loves to hear from her readers. You can write to her at P.O. Box 524, Bellevue, WA 98009, U.S.A. Or visit her Web site at www.janeporter.com.

For Ty and our new baby boy, Mac Bran Gumey.

It's going to be a wonderful Christmas!

PROLOGUE

Monte Carlo

SHEIKH ZAYED FEHR, the middle brother of the three powerful Fehrs, read the letter yet again. It had been typed on the heavy ivory parchment of the royal Fehr family but the correspondence came from Khalid, the youngest brother, instead of eldest brother, Sharif, the king.

The letter was short and uncomplicated. Khalid's words were simple enough.

Zayed's hand shook.

He blinked. He, Zayed Fehr, the heartless Fehr, could barely breathe. Pain hot and hard and sharp exploded in his chest once, twice and again. He exhaled against the shock of it.

Khalid had to be wrong. Khalid was mistaken. Surely if this were true Zayed would have heard something on the news, heard something before this formal letter.

It just couldn't be.

Couldn't.

And Zayed, the heartless, knew for the first time in

fifteen years he wasn't heartless because his was breaking now.

Sharif, his beloved big brother, was missing. His plane had crashed somewhere in the Sahara Desert and he was presumed dead.

Effective immediately, Zayed needed to marry and come home.

Because Sharif's son was three and not of age to rule, Zayed would be king.

CHAPTER ONE

Vancouver, Canada

"SHEIKH ZAYED FEHR is *here*? In Vancouver?" Dr. Rou Tornell repeated, her hand shaking ever so slightly as she removed her glasses to rub the bridge of her nose.

She told herself it was fatigue making her hand tremble; exhaustion was only to be expected after a seven-week book tour.

She told herself it had nothing, absolutely nothing, to do with Sheikh Zayed Fehr, the younger brother of King Sharif Fehr, and the only man who'd ever hurt or humiliated her the way he had.

Jamie, Rou's assistant, moved forward toward the desk where Rou was working on her laptop, concern creasing her brow. "Yes. He's…here."

"What do you mean, *here*?" Rou demanded, her normally cool voice now wobbling with shock.

"I mean, here. In this hotel."

"What?" Rou shoved the glasses back on her nose and stared at Jamie in consternation. She normally wore contact lenses for appearances but in the privacy of her hotel suite she preferred the comfort of glasses. *"Why?"*

"You told him you didn't have time to see him in Portland. Or Seattle. So he's flown to Vancouver and he's here now." Jamie smiled nervously, hands fidgeting. "And I don't think he's going to go away until you see him. Apparently it's urgent. Life or death, or something of that nature."

Life or death. Just the sort of thing her father would say. Zayed was cut from the same cloth. Gorgeous, wealthy, famous, shallow and self-absorbed. It was always about them, what they wanted, what they needed. She despised playboys and movie stars, loathed self-indulgence, and loathed Zayed Fehr most of all.

Zayed might be Sharif's brother, but he was truly the black sheep of the family. A desert prince without a care, or sense of responsibility, or propriety, for that matter. Rou gestured unhappily. "I don't have time to see him—"

"You do now, actually—"

"But I don't want to see him."

"Have you ever seen him?" twenty-three-year-old Jamie asked breathlessly.

"We're acquainted," Rou answered flatly, unwilling to admit to more than that. Jamie certainly didn't need to know the details of their painful, embarrassing encounter three years earlier. Suffice it to say that Zayed Fehr would never be a man she respected, or trusted.

"He is really good-looking," Jamie added, eyes bright and cheeks pink.

"He is," Rou answered with an exasperated sigh. "He might even be physical perfection. He also has an ungodly amount of money, a shocking amount of power, but that doesn't make him a good person."

Jamie's shoulders lifted and fell. "He seems nice enough. Actually, he seems very nice—"

"You've seen him?"

"Well, yes. He's *here*. In the outer room."

"In my hotel suite?"

Jamie's blush deepened. "I told him he could wait there. I thought perhaps you had five minutes now. The media escort won't be here for another half hour and they're doing your makeup at the TV station." She saw Rou's expression and hurriedly added, "He really is desperate to see you."

Rou shuffled the papers before her, trying to cover her panic. Zayed here, now? Zayed outside her door, waiting in her suite?

"Did I do something wrong?" Jamie asked nervously.

Yes, she wanted to shout. "No," she answered instead, swallowing hard even as she became aware that her hands were damp and her heart racing.

She was also aware that Jamie was suddenly close to tears, and the last thing she wanted—needed— was Jamie crying. Jamie tried so hard, and was a lovely girl and usually an efficient assistant. Rou couldn't blame her for falling under Zayed's spell. Zayed wasn't just gorgeous and rich, he was also charming and charismatic and women fell at his feet. Even she—cool, logical scientist—had fallen at his feet.

"I thought you'd have five minutes," Jamie stammered.

Rou pressed her hands to the desk edge to stop their trembling. Of course she did. That wasn't the problem. The problem was, she didn't want to spare Zayed Fehr five minutes. She didn't want to see him. Not even for five seconds. "How long has he been waiting?" she asked as silence stretched.

Jamie's pink cheeks grew rosier. "A half hour."

Rou blanched inwardly, although years of experience as a therapist allowed her to remain expressionless. "Why didn't you tell me earlier?"

"I…" Jamie's shoulders lifted and fell. "I…"

"Never mind. It's all right." Rou squared her slim shoulders and tucked long, fine blond hair behind one ear. "Send him in. I'll see him. But five minutes. That's all he gets." Her voice firmed and her chin lifted. "Make sure he understands."

Zayed stood in the suite's outer room waiting to be admitted to see Rou Tornell, bestselling author, international speaker and professional matchmaker.

It was the professional matchmaker part that made his upper lip curl ever so slightly.

Who would have ever thought that Sharif's timid little protégée would end up an international speaker, never mind an exclusive, professional matchmaker?

Who would have thought that introverted, academic Rou Tornell would understand sexual attraction, much less romantic attachment?

Zayed was usually too chivalrous to make comparisons among women, but with Rou Tornell it was impossible not to. She was the coldest, stiffest, stuffiest woman he'd ever met, and while Sharif said she was merely focused, Zayed's experience made him suspect she was seriously repressed, maybe even clinically depressed.

If it weren't for Sharif, he wouldn't be here today.

But then who would have ever imagined that Sharif, just four years older than him, would disappear? Who would have thought the Fehr royal jet would crash?

Zayed's eyes closed briefly as ungodly pain ripped through his chest. The pain felt even hotter and more vivid now than it had been when he'd first received the news five days ago. Since then he'd flown home to Sarq to see his youngest brother, Khalid, who was trying to keep things together until Zayed could return and take over.

Zayed had also spent time with Sharif's queen, Jesslyn, and the children. Four children all stunned and grieving, missing their adored father.

It was worse at the palace than he'd imagined. The grief, the fear, the heartbreak. No one knew what had happened. It was as if the plane had just fallen from the sky. No warning, no signal of distress, no radio call for help. The plane was just gone. Tomorrow it'd be a week since the disappearance.

On day fourteen, by law, Zayed would inherit the throne.

It was impossible. Zayed was not a ruler, or a leader. He did not belong in Sarq. The desert was no longer in his blood. He craved rain, not sun. Skyscrapers and penthouses were now home.

But Jesslyn's face—her eyes so haunted—remained with him. As did Khalid's silent, endless grief. And maybe it was this that pierced his heart.

I need you, Khalid had whispered as they hugged goodbye. *We all need you. Come home.*

Khalid had never asked Zayed for anything. None of them had ever asked Zayed for anything. Sharif was the one they had all turned to. Sharif was the eldest, the rock, the center of the family.

But now…now…Sharif was gone.

Just like that.

No wonder Jesslyn looked like a ghost. No wonder Khalid hadn't slept in days. Their world was turned upside down. Nothing would ever be the same.

The door to the suite's living room opened and Jamie, the young personal assistant, pretty and a little plump, stepped out and closed the door behind her.

"Dr. Tornell can meet with you now," she said, round cheeks darkening with a rush of color. "But I'm afraid she's on a tight schedule as she has several media appearances this afternoon before tonight's book signing so it'll be for just a few minutes."

"Not a problem," he answered easily, thinking it was already so very Rou Tornell. Busy, busy, busy. So very self-important. He checked his smile as he followed the assistant through the door into the living room.

He'd taken just a few steps into the room when he spotted Rou at a corner desk in the lovely sitting room, a laptop open before her. She was wearing glasses today, her long blond hair unceremoniously tucked behind her ears. Blond, thin, bookish and tense, Rou Tornell exuded the warmth of an ice cube. Her personality was about as interesting. But she was successful, and reputedly the best in her field, and that's what he needed.

The assistant disappeared, discreetly closing the door behind her.

"Good afternoon, Sheikh Fehr," Rou greeted him as the door shut. "I'm in a bit of a rush, but I understand from Jamie that you're apparently desperate to see me."

Her frosty tone didn't escape him and his lips compressed. *Forget ice cube, try iceberg,* he thought cynically, realizing she hadn't changed, and she never would. "I wouldn't say desperate, Dr. Tornell. Determined is probably more accurate."

She leaned back in her chair, folded her hands together, her gaze stony. "I can't imagine how I might be of service to you," she added coolly, hating how her pulse was already too quick.

She didn't like him. She'd never like him. And the only reason she'd agreed to see him today was out of courtesy to Sharif.

"It's been a while," he said, approaching. "Two years?"

"Three." Rou felt a jolt as Zayed neared. He was

even more magnetic than she'd remembered; she'd forgotten how he owned a room, how he seemed to become the room. And then there was his height, and his build, and how his clothes had been tailored to lovingly drape him. Her father had owned a room the same way, but then her father had been one of the greatest film stars of his day.

But Zayed was no film star, nor pop star. He was a sheikh who acted more Western than the most Western man. A sheikh with billions of his own, never mind his family's fortune, a man who did what he pleased, when he pleased, and how he pleased. Even if he hurt others in the process.

Her jaw tightened and she flexed her fingers ever so slightly.

It still vexed her that he had hurt her. She shouldn't have let a man like him have that kind of power. But then, she hadn't thought he did.

Yet there was a positive that came out of the painful and humiliating episode. It was the insight she gleaned into his character, insight which became her second bestselling book, *He's No Prince: Detecting the Bad Boys, Players & Con Artists So You Can Find True Love*.

"That long?" he answered with an equally cool smile. "It seems like just yesterday when we first met."

"Does it? Probably not to Pippa. She's had two babies since." Rou's gaze met his and held, even as her stomach squeezed into knots. God, she hated him. Hated that he'd hurt her, hated that he'd mocked her, hated that he'd made her realize she would never trust men, and never find true love of her own.

"Two for Lady Pippa? She's been busy, hasn't she?"

And just like that, Rou flashed back to the weekend they'd first met at her client Lady Pippa Collins's wedding in Winchester. Sharif was to have been there, but at the last moment he couldn't attend, and apparently his younger brother the Prince Zayed Fehr of Sarq had taken his place.

Pippa had been the one to introduce them during the reception. "Sheikh Fehr," Pippa had said, stopping Rou in front of the sheikh's table, "I couldn't let you leave without meeting my dear friend Rou Tornell."

Zayed Fehr had risen to his feet, and it was the most regal, elegant rise Rou had ever seen.

Like Sharif, he was tall, very tall, with broad shoulders and a narrow waist and at full height he stood easily a full head and a half taller than Rou, and she wasn't short. And while Sharif was handsome, Zayed was alarmingly, unnervingly good-looking. Dark gold eyes. Jet-black hair. Smooth jaw not quite square but distinctly male, and it balanced his strong nose and high cheekbones. They were, she thought rather dizzily, cheekbones that a model would kill for. He must photograph beautifully. But then, he was model beautiful in person. Part of her knew she could never really trust him, as beautiful men were the most savage and selfish of all, but another part of her wanted to like him because he was, after all, Sharif's brother.

"It's because of Rou that we are all here," Pippa added, beaming and patting Rou's arm. "My darling Rou introduced me to Henry a year ago."

Sheikh Fehr's eyes had narrowed, gleamed, creases fanning at the corners of those magnificent eyes. The first sign that he wasn't a lad of twenty, but a man in his prime, probably somewhere around thirty-two or thirty-three.

"How fortuitous," he said, the corner of his mouth lifting in the driest, most mocking voice Rou had ever heard. And she'd heard plenty. She was a psychologist after all.

Rou stiffened, but Pippa was oblivious, too giddy with happiness, and the bride smiled radiantly at the sheikh. "Rou—Dr. Tornell—has a true gift. I am—can you believe it?—her hundredth wedding. She's introduced one hundred couples now, couples that all ended up in marriage." Pippa turned to Rou. "I got it right, didn't I?" And then ecstatic Pippa was off, as her new husband was gesturing for her to join him, which left Rou alone with the sheikh.

But then, to her surprise, Zayed had invited her to join him at his table, and somehow they'd spent the rest of the evening together. They'd talked for hours, and then danced, and then later they'd left the wedding reception and gone across the street to the little hotel bar and had a nightcap together.

She remembered everything about that night. The

warmth of his body as they danced. The seductive red walls of the hotel bar. The balloon glass of orange liqueur that she'd cradled in her hands.

Zayed's attention had been dazzling. He'd listened to her, laughed at her nervous jokes, talked about his work and a few of his recent investments, including a new resort on the coast in his country, Sarq.

Those hours together were delicious. It'd been ages since she'd been on a date, much less with a man like Zayed Fehr who made her feel beautiful and fascinating. She'd fallen for him, and she sensed he'd fallen for her, too. As he put her into a cab late that night, he'd brushed his lips across her cheek and she'd been sure, so sure, he'd call her for a real date, and soon.

But Zayed didn't call. And she would have never known how he really felt about her if Sharif hadn't accidentally sent her an e-mail that wasn't meant for her. He'd meant to reply to Zayed. Instead he'd somehow sent it to her. Sharif caught his mistake before she did, phoning to apologize, phoning to beg her forgiveness, phoning to plead that she just delete the offending e-mail without reading it.

But Rou, ever curious, read the e-mail instead.

Spending the evening with her was like a night at a museum of science—dull, dull, dull, but you get through it by convincing yourself you're doing a good deed. More unfortunately, I could tell she liked me but obviously the attraction wasn't mutual. She has all the warmth and charm of a department store mannequin.

"You're still matchmaking," Zayed said now, dropping into a chair opposite her desk.

A department store mannequin, Rou silently repeated, her cheeks burning at the memory. *Dull, dull, dull.* Her hands trembled in her lap. "Yes," she said flatly, hating that his appearance had brought all those feelings back, too. The only saving grace was that Zayed didn't know she knew about his e-mail to Sharif. Sharif had promised her that. "So what can I do for you, Sheikh Fehr?"

"You would know why I'm here if you had listened to my calls," he said pleasantly. "I believe I left half a dozen messages for you. Never mind the e-mails."

She eyed him for a long moment. He was dressed in an exquisitely tailored suit and white shirt—no tie—and his dark hair was cut shorter than it had been three years ago, better showing off the ideal shape of his head; the strong jaw; the long, straight nose; elegant cheekbones; and the eyes, golden eyes. "I've been traveling," she answered shortly.

"Perhaps you need better technology."

Her eyes narrowed. "So why are you here?"

"I'm thirty-six. I'd like a wife."

Rou stared at him waiting for the punch line. Because it was a joke. Zayed Fehr, celebrated bachelor, Monte Carlo's richest, most famous, reckless playboy, wanted a wife? She couldn't stifle her laugh.

He didn't crack a smile. He simply stared back at her, his gaze steady, never once blinking.

"What can I really do for you, Sheikh Fehr?"

"You could pull out your paperwork, that pile of forms you use and begin to fill them out. The name is Fehr, F-e-h-r. Zayed is the first name. Do you need me to spell that, too?"

"No." She gritted her teeth at his tone as well as his voice. His voice was just as she'd remembered. Deep and smooth, so husky as to be almost caressing.

No wonder women fell.

No wonder she'd fallen.

How stupid she'd been to fall.

Old shame sharpened her voice. "Why a wife, why now? You've made it clear for years you're not a fan of marriage—"

"Things have changed." His voice changed, deepened. "It's not an option. Not anymore. Not if I'm to assume the throne in Sarq. It is Sarq law. No man shall inherit the throne before twenty-five, and when he does assume rule, he must be married. The king must have a wife."

"You're marrying so you can be king?"

"It is Sarq law."

She studied him, puzzled. Sharif was king of Sarq. She knew that, everyone knew that. But perhaps there was another country, or a Sarq desert tribe in need of a feudal king. She knew she was missing key pieces of information, but as Zayed hadn't volunteered the information she wasn't going to probe. The less she knew of him the better. "I am sure you could find an agreeable wife if you wanted one badly enough—"

"I'm in a hurry."

"I see." Her voice dripped sarcasm. But she didn't see. She didn't understand anything other than he was awful and she wanted him gone. Who did he think he was? And why did he think he could show up here after three years and demand her assistance? How could any man be more shallow or selfish?

"So you'll do it?" Zayed pressed.

"No. Absolutely not." And she didn't feel bad in the least. In fact, she rather enjoyed her position of power. "Marriage can't be rushed. Finding a suitable life partner takes time and careful study. And secondly, you're not suitable—"

"I'm not what?"

She ignored his interruption. "—as a candidate for my practice. That's not to say you couldn't find a willing candidate if you did some legwork of your own."

He smiled at her, all white straight teeth and gleaming eyes, but it wasn't a friendly expression. "But I don't want a willing candidate, Dr. Tornell, or an agreeable wife. If that were the case, I'd allow my mother to pick my bride. I don't want just any bride, I want the right wife. That is why I am here. You are the relationship expert. You can find the right woman for me."

"But I can't," she answered ruthlessly. "Sorry." But not in the least sorry. She'd never find him a wife.

She'd never help him. She'd never doom a woman to a life sentence with him.

And suddenly she thought of her own mother, the famous British model, a woman the world admired and envied, and yet a woman who couldn't make her father happy.

A tap sounded on the door and Jamie stepped inside to gesture to her watch. Rou glanced at her own watch. Fifteen minutes had already passed. The media escort would be here in fifteen to escort her to the TV station and Rou still needed to change and freshen her hair. She rose, fingers pressed to the surface of the desk. "If you'll excuse me, Sheikh Fehr, I must get ready for my next appointment—"

"Is this because of Angela Moss?"

Rou froze. "I don't know—"

"She was your client. A year ago. Surely you remember her? Slim, striking redhead. Twenty-six years old. Former model turned purse designer. Ring a bell?"

Of course Rou remembered Angela.

The sheikh had wooed her, won her and then cast her aside within months, and because of Rou's personal feelings about Zayed, she'd refused to take Angela on as a client, but then Angela had tried to take her life, and Rou realized she had to help the poor girl. Angela was beyond desperate, and even with Rou's help, it took months of patience and skill to walk her new client through the heartbreak.

When still in the chemical rush of love, having

one's heart broken is a form of death. For others, it's like detox. The brain, suddenly starved of the opiates that had previously fed it, craves the beloved, needing contact, needing that flood of chemicals and hormones that comes with togetherness.

After twelve years of research she understood that love, falling in love, was the most potent drug man would ever know. Love was maddening, delicious, addictive. And when it went wrong, destructive.

"I know she came to you," Zayed added tonelessly. "I was the one who gave her your name. I thought you could help her."

Rou sank back down into her chair. "*You* sent her to me?" She gave her head a slow disbelieving shake. "Why?"

His brow furrowed and he lifted his hands as if the answer was self-explanatory. "I was worried about her."

"So you do have a conscience."

"I didn't love her, but I didn't want her hurt."

She eyed him with disdain. "Then maybe you should stop seeing women with hearts and brains."

One black eyebrow lifted. "What are you suggesting?"

"Puppets. Robots. Rag dolls. Blow-up dolls." She smiled thinly. "They won't be hurt when you cast them aside."

There was a flicker in his eyes—surprise, maybe— and then it was gone. "You're angry."

Rou realized Jamie was still hovering in the doorway and she gestured for her to give them five more minutes. Once Jamie was gone, Rou looked at him. "I'm not angry. I just don't have any need for you."

"Need?" he drawled.

"Let me be clearer." She leaned forward, her gaze intent on his. "I don't particularly like you, Sheikh Fehr, and because my practice is very successful and very busy I can afford to be selective. Therefore, I'd never work with you."

"Why not?"

"Why not, what?"

"Why won't you work with me?"

"I already said—"

"No, you're giving personal opinions. I want a professional opinion. You are a scientist, are you not?"

God, he was arrogant. "I know too much about you. I couldn't approach your situation without prejudice—"

"Because I didn't love Angela?"

"Because you don't love. You can't love," she blurted, before grinding her teeth together in remorse. She wasn't supposed to say that last bit. It was something Angela had told her. Angela had said that Zayed had used his inability to love as the reason to end their relationship. Apparently he didn't love, couldn't love—seemed he'd never been in love—and because he couldn't love, he thought it best to end their relationship as Angela's feelings had grown too strong.

Classic narcissist.

Her father had never loved anyone but himself, either. Narcissists couldn't love anyone else. Couldn't see anyone else as separate or having individual needs.

"I'm sorry," she added. "That was inappropriate of me. Doctor-patient confidentiality. But you can see why I can't work with you. After counseling Angela, after knowing certain things about you, I believe it'd be too much of a conflict of interest."

He looked at her levelly. "Of whose interest?"

"Yours."

"And this is all based on my six dates with Angela?"

No, she answered silently, *it's also based on my personal experience with you.* But she didn't say that, as she'd never let him know she was aware of what he really thought of her. "It's not complicated, Sheikh Fehr. You're being deliberately obtuse." Her voice hardened. "You told Angela you'd never marry. You said you'd never fallen in love, and that you were unable to love, and therefore, you didn't believe you could be loyal to any woman—"

"I've changed." His lashes lifted and the light golden gaze met hers.

"That's not possible."

"Isn't it?" His gaze skewered her. "You are a psychologist, aren't you?"

Jamie's head appeared around the corner of the door. "I'm sorry to interrupt again, but your escort's arrived, Dr. Tornell. She's waiting in the lobby."

Rou nodded at Jamie and yet she never took her eyes off Zayed. She waited for the door to close. "I have to go."

"Time is of the essence, so let's meet for dinner. We'll start tonight. The profile, the background information, everything—"

"No." She rose to her feet, wound more tightly than she could ever remember. "Never."

"Never?"

"It wouldn't be right. I couldn't represent you fairly, and—" she took a deep breath "—I'm not sure I'd want to."

"I'm not asking you to find a cure for cancer, Dr. Tornell. I'm asking you to find me a wife."

She moved from the desk. "You might as well ask me to find a cure. It'd be easier."

If she'd hoped to quell him, she'd failed, as he laughed a deep bitter laugh. "I thought you were a professional."

"I am."

"Then do your job. It's what you're good at, and apparently the only thing you're good at."

Her breath caught as though she'd been sucker punched. "That's low, and mean-spirited."

"And you haven't been? You judged and sentenced me before even meeting with me today. Fine. I don't need your approval, but I need your time and your skill."

"If you did your research you'd know that I don't just accept everyone as a client. I take less than five percent of the applicants that come to me. My success is based on the fact that I'm exclusive. I only work with people I believe I can help."

"And you could help me. I have an entire country

waiting for me to return. Do this and I promise you that you will be compensated handsomely."

"This isn't about money. It's about values and ethics, and working with you goes against my ethics, and frankly, no amount of money could induce me to compromise—"

"Not even five million pounds?"

For a moment she didn't speak, not sure she'd heard him correctly. "Five million pounds?" she finally repeated, even as she mentally translated it to eight million American dollars. Eight million American dollars. "That's ridiculous. I've never charged anything close to that, and I'd never accept a figure like that. The very offer smacks of desperation."

"Determination," he corrected. "And it's sufficient compensation for you to overcome your objections, don't you think?"

"No! I don't care about money," she spat, her patience shot. "I don't do what I do for money. It's never been about money. I do it for... I do it because..." But her voice failed her. The words wouldn't come. She couldn't say it, couldn't tell him why she did what she did. It was far too personal for a man like Zayed, a man who didn't care about anyone or anything but himself.

"Then don't think of it as money. Think of it as funding for your research center, the one you've been wanting to open in Oakland for the past several years. Find me a wife I can take to Sarq as my queen, and you have your facility. I can't think of a fairer bargain.

I get what I want, and you get what you want, and everyone is better off."

"But I don't know that anyone would be better off—"

"Isn't that the problem? You don't know," he said, almost gently, as he got to his feet. "You don't know me. You think you do. But you don't." His golden gaze held hers, challenging her. "Perhaps you could do a little research before you jump to any conclusions. Just as I did my research before I came to you."

He was moving to the door, about to walk out when Rou stopped him. "So what did your research turn up, Sheikh Fehr?"

He paused in the doorway, looked at her. "I know why you're so rigid and repressed. I know why you're more machine than woman. It has nothing to do with money, and everything to do with your parents' divorce. It broke your heart, didn't it?"

She was speechless. He knew. No one knew. She'd never told anyone. How could he know?

He tipped his head. "You have an appearance at Fireside Books tonight at seven. I'll pick you up from there at nine. Good luck with your interview." And he was gone.

CHAPTER TWO

BUT she wasn't at Fireside Books when he arrived, a half hour before the signing was to have ended. She'd cut the event short, citing illness, and she'd left.

Zayed rocked back on his heels as he stood outside the bookstore digesting the information. It was a crisp night and the late-October wind sent red and gold leaves swirling past his feet.

The ice maiden had run rather than meet with him.

That was a first, and certainly a change from how attentive she'd been at Lady Pippa's wedding three years ago. That night Rou Tornell had clung to him like Velcro, hanging on his every word. But then, women were forever throwing themselves at him, eager, so eager, to be his next lover.

Fortunately, he'd always treated his women well—Angela included. Even after the relationship had ended, Zayed made sure the women were okay. Financially. Emotionally. He might be hard, but he wasn't a complete ass. He had had sisters, after all.

Zayed pulled his phone from his pocket, knowing already that Rou Tornell would no longer be found at the Fairmont. If she'd left the store early, he suspected she'd left town early, and not for San Francisco, which was her home, but to Austria where she'd be attending another one of her high-profile weddings in just two days. Which was perfect, actually. He'd been invited to Ralf and Princess Georgina's wedding, too.

I now pronounce you man and wife.

The guests erupted into applause as the groom lifted Georgina's veil and dipped his head and bent her back over his arm to kiss her, her silk gown sparkling with the five thousand crystals hand stitched across the delicate fabric.

The kiss ended, and the couple turned to face the congregation, and Rou's breath caught in her throat at the expression on Georgina's face. She was so happy, so deeply in love and it struck Rou that while St. Stephan's Cathedral glowed with candlelight and the glittering guests, none shone more brightly than Georgina herself.

The light in Georgina's eyes alone made Rou's heart ache.

Rou's heart turned over as music swelled, filling the grand Gothic cathedral as the beaming bride and groom walked down the aisle. *Georgina's found her match. She's found her mate.*

Weddings always moved her, but this one, this was exceptional. Georgina had been hurt so badly three years ago when her fiancé left her at the altar and she'd sworn off men, sworn off love, sworn off being a wife and mother.

Rou, Georgina's childhood friend, refused to accept that one of her oldest, dearest friends would never have a happy ending, and she'd worked quietly behind the scenes looking for the right man. And then she'd found him. Baron Ralf van Kliesen, an Austrian count by title, born and raised in the Australian Outback by his Australian mother. Ralf was perfect for Georgina— strong, independent, handsome, brilliant, but kind, very kind, and that was what Georgina needed most. A strong yet tender man to love her. Forever.

Forever.

The lump in Rou's throat grew and spread, pressing hot and heavy on her chest, and up behind her eyes so they stung with brilliant unshed tears.

To be loved forever. To love forever. To be so blessed.

As a young girl, Rou had once felt safe and loved, but when her parents' marriage changed, it changed so dramatically, so violently, their lives were never the same again. Worse, because her parents were so famous, their divorce and destructiveness played out in the media, their battles gossip fodder, their phone calls taped and played for the press. They both fought hard for custody. They both claimed they wanted Rou, needed her, must have her. But neither truly wanted her. They just didn't want the other one to win.

Love wasn't about winning, and love wasn't abuse. Love was generous and kind. Respectful. Supportive. And this was why Rou did what she did—matched couples by values, beliefs, needs. Not by externals like appearances, although appearances counted. People fell in love with an image, but there had to be something behind the image. There had to be a real connection, a genuine understanding.

Rou was still more emotional than she liked when she exited the cathedral, descending the stone steps to the street. The moon was already yellow in the sky and even in the city the autumn night smelled of crackling leaves and a brisk hungry wind.

Climbing into her waiting limousine, she pressed the collar of her soft velvet cloak to her throat. The rich crush of the material warmed her. It was such an extravagant thing, lined with black silk, the silver clasp studded with genuine diamonds. It had been her mother's cape, bought to accompany her father to a premiere of one of his movies. Rou remembered the framed photo of her mother and father on the red carpet, her mother smiling her dazzling smile, the cape snug about her shoulders.

The photo was long gone—burned, just as her mother had destroyed all the clothes she'd worn while married, cutting some, burning others. But the cape escaped. It'd been left in England after one of her mother's trips back home, and it'd hung in Grandmother's closet forgotten until Rou found it at sixteen, two years after her mother's death.

The limousine had arrived at the palace, and inside she checked her cherished cloak, and turning toward the ballroom, hesitated for just a moment before the doors, aware she was alone, aware she'd turn no heads, but also grateful for her anonymity. Her parents' beauty bewitched the world. Rou dazzled no one. But it was also better this way. She could live quietly. And she could remain in control. Control being very important to her well-being.

With a quick hand over her hip, she smoothed the jersey fabric of her conservative black gown and entered the gold-and-white ballroom illuminated by a thousand gleaming candles.

And the first person she spotted across the ballroom was Zayed Fehr.

She froze.

Couldn't be, she told herself, stepping back as if she could escape into the shadows. Instead she bumped into a waiter and spilled one of the glasses of champagne he carried.

She apologized profusely in German, and glanced over at Zayed Fehr again.

It was him. Had to be him. No one else looked like that, or moved like that. And God help her, it appeared he was coming toward her.

Panicked, Rou disappeared into the crowd and then fled the ballroom for the hall where she retreated to the elegant ivory-and-gold ladies' room.

Rou paced the lounge area of the ladies' room, so agitated she chewed on a knuckle, something she never ever did.

What was he doing here? Why would he be here? Oh, but she knew the answer to that. He'd wanted her help. She'd refused. So he'd hunted her down here. Damn him.

For twenty minutes, she hid in the ladies' room

until she heard the trumpets herald the arrival of Ralf and Georgina. Surely Zayed would be gone by now.

But she was wrong. She'd taken only four steps into the high-ceilinged hall before he appeared before her, blocking her access to the ballroom.

"How did your Vancouver event go?" he asked conversationally, as if they were old friends, good friends.

Rou's mouth dried even as her pulse jumped. She couldn't have answered him if she tried. Instead she longed for her cloak, to bury herself inside the comfort of velvet and hide.

"I heard from the store owner that it was a smaller turnout than expected," he added. "Were you disappointed?"

Her eyes snapped at him. "No."

"So the lackluster turnout wasn't why you hightailed it out of town?"

Rou hated that she blushed, but she couldn't help it. She didn't know if she was blushing because he'd discovered that her event had been less than stellar, or if it was because he'd actually turned up at the store as he'd said he would, and by the time he showed, she'd already taken off, rushing for Vancouver Airport to catch her flight to Munich and then on to Vienna. "I can't believe you chased me all the way from Vancouver to Vienna."

"I was invited to the wedding, and I wouldn't use the word *chase*—"

"No, you would say you were being persistent," she flashed bitterly.

Zayed nearly smiled. "Or determined," he agreed.

"But I am determined, and once I've set my mind on something I always succeed. You must know that you're making this more difficult than it needs to be."

He was wearing a tuxedo with tails, and the jacket hugged his broad chest, tapering at the waist. He looked sinful, darkly handsome, his golden eyes intense in that striking face.

She averted her own eyes, pretending to watch those still arriving. "The only difficulty is your inability to accept rejection."

"That's not quite correct, Dr. Tornell. In Vancouver you led me to believe there was a possibility of us working together. You did agree to meet me after your event, and I was there. I waited for you. And when you didn't emerge from the store, I went in looking for you. The owner was there. The cashier. Your media escort. A couple of readers still lingering in the afterglow. But you, you were long gone."

She studied one couple disappearing into an alcove, arms entwined, eager to touch, to be alone. Early love was like that. A craving for contact, a craving for skin. She couldn't imagine such an intense physical need. She'd never felt a physical need.

With an effort she turned her attention back to Zayed. "I have already made commitments to others, clients currently under contract. I don't think it would be fair to them to take on someone new right now."

"And yet you just met with a prospective client this morning, and I believe she walked away under the assumption that you would take her on?"

Rou rarely blushed and yet again heat surged to her cheeks, her face burning from her chin to her brow. Her thoughts were just as chaotic. For some reason she couldn't think when Zayed Fehr was near. All her logical thought disappeared in a puff of panic, a cloud of emotion. And Rou didn't trust emotion. "Are you spying on me?"

"I don't spy, but I do have bodyguards and personal assistants. Butlers, chauffeurs and valets—"

"I get the picture," she said stiffly, "and for a man so powerful, I can't help but wonder why you chose me to help with your search for a queen."

"You're successful. And your matches endure. I've yet to hear of one marriage ending in divorce."

Rou felt a shiver race through her. The very word *divorce* made her cold. Divorce. Attorneys. Judges. Courtrooms. Nasty, hateful, deceitful allegations. Seven years it'd taken her parents to finalize everything. Seven years. And by the time they finally had an agreement in place, they'd destroyed everything and everyone, including their own daughter.

It had taken Rou all of her teens and well into her twenties to heal, and the only reason she did heal was her friendship with Sharif Fehr. He'd made sure she returned to school, made sure she had the funds to continue through graduate school. With his financial support, she'd been able to keep her vow that she'd work to make sure that no child, and no family, should ever suffer the way she had.

Chilled, Rou thought of her soft velvet cape in the

cloakroom and then of her cozy hotel room at the exquisite Hotel Bristol. She was ready to return to her room, ready for the safety and warmth the four walls provided. "It's late and I'm still very jet-lagged...."

"Running away again, Dr. Tornell? And yet aren't you the expert at teaching women to stand their ground, and face their fears, and look reality in the eye?"

"Yes. But I'm also the expert who says women should trust their gut, and my gut says you are dangerous."

He laughed, and his laughter silenced her.

He should have been appalled, angered, but no, he laughed.

She lifted her chin. "I'm deadly serious, Sheikh Fehr."

"I'm sure you are, but you're so wrong in this case, so completely off base, that I can't help but wonder if you're really a scientist or if those are someone else's degrees from Cambridge tacked on after your name."

"I assure you, I've earned every doctoral degree, thank you."

He smiled, but his eyes were cold. "Then act like a scientist, because that's what I want. I'm most certainly not interested in the woman in you."

"That's good, because the woman in me despises the man in you."

She walked away then, legs shaking with every step. She felt ill. *Exposed.* Any other time she would have left the reception, but this night was Georgina's night and she couldn't leave, not yet, not until dinner was over and the dancing began.

Zayed let her walk, watching her slim, black-clad figure disappear through the ballroom doors toward the dinner tables.

She's changed, he reflected, as she faded into the crowd.

Three years ago she was a chatterbox—nervous, tense and gawky. Now she had more polish—her success, maybe?—but she was far colder, and harder. Interesting how time and success changed one.

But her brittle hardness didn't deter him. He needed her. Time was running short, and his intensely meddlesome mother was already starting her matchmaking, and God kew he didn't want a traditional Sarq girl. He knew himself and feared he'd destroy such a woman in no time. Girls in Sarq were still raised to be meek and mild, compliant and acquiescing. A young Sarq woman wouldn't know how to converse with him, or argue properly. She'd simply nod and say, Yes, my lord. Yes, my love, yes.

How he'd hate that. How he'd hate a partner that wasn't strong, wasn't an equal. But finding an equal in his world was next to impossible. He wasn't ugly, far from it, and that was the problem. Women saw his face and they all found it tragically well put together. They heard his name. Learned of his title, his power, his staggering wealth and they all fell, tumbling to his feet, so eager. Too eager.

He couldn't marry a woman like that, either.

He wouldn't trust or respect a woman like that. And without trust or respect, he'd soon be irritated, which would make lovemaking a chore, dooming the relationship.

Zayed was many things, and he'd broken many rules and many laws, but even he believed marriage to be sacred. He'd never slept with a married woman. And he'd never cheat on his wife.

So he needed the right wife. The perfect wife.

And frigid, rigid Rou Tornell might lack charm and personality, but she was supremely skilled at match-making. And he was determined she'd find him a match.

He followed her.

She'd just taken her seat at the dinner table. It was assigned seating and he wasn't at her table, but he pulled out a chair next to her and sat down anyway.

She turned her head and shot him a furious, frosty look. "Go away."

He shrugged, smiled carelessly and leaned closer, his broad shoulders crowding her. "I can't, Dr. Tornell. I need your help."

She averted her head, apparently watching the guests in mute fascination.

They were a stellar bunch, he acknowledged, a dazzling mix of royalty, international aristocrats, celebrities and socialites—all dressed as if they had personal stylists, and most, he suspected, did.

Rou was perhaps the only one who looked as if she'd dressed herself. His gaze flickered over her sedate black gown. It seemed painfully familiar, and he wondered if it was the same black gown she'd worn to Lady Pippa's wedding three years earlier.

"Isn't this the same dress you wore three years ago?" he asked now.

She turned her head, cheeks suffused with color. "Yes. Why? You don't like it?"

He'd scored a direct hit, he thought, observing the emotions flashing across her face. And in that moment, she looked almost pretty, her eyes dark, her cheeks deep pink, her lips trembling with outrage. "You could probably find a more flattering style and color," he answered.

Her lips compressed and her gaze leveled on his. "Black is always in style."

"No, not true, especially when black makes you appear sallow. You'd do better in pinks."

"For your information, this is a designer gown of good fabric which I bought at Barney's in New York—"

"Ten years ago, I imagine from the look of the sleeves."

Her eyes widened, the blue irises almost black with fury. "Go away," she said.

"I can't."

"Can't or won't?"

The air caught in Rou's throat as he turned more fully toward her, his shoulder grazing hers. "Both."

He was so close to her she could see shots of bronze against the gold of his eyes and faint creases at the edges of his eyes. His body was big, sinewy, and his thigh brushed hers until she dragged her own legs farther away.

"I've already told you, I'd never help you," she answered, aware that her pulse had quickened and her body felt warm and dangerously sensitive.

"That's because you're making my request personal, but it's not personal. It's so much bigger than that. This is about my country. My brother. My people. You hold an entire country hostage right now."

He leaned closer, so that his head was just inches from hers and his arm stretched along the back of her chair, his fingers dangerously close to her skin. "All I want is the same opportunity you've given your other clients. Do the preliminary assessment properly. Do the paperwork, the background research. I will make my life available to you. I am at your disposal for the next however many weeks it takes to complete the process."

She'd stiffened in protest when he moved even closer, breathing deeply to calm herself, but breathing deeply meant she inhaled his fragrance—the scent soft, spicy, seductive—and she wasn't sure if it was his scent, or his warmth, but her nerves clamored to life and her senses swam.

She felt as though she were drowning at sea. And he was doing it to her. He was overwhelming her, threatening her very safety. She couldn't allow it. She couldn't. He made her feel as if her own survival was at stake, too.

And survival was not to be taken lightly.

She'd known he was dangerous from their first meeting at Pippa's wedding, and yet she'd danced with him anyway and even gone and sat in the hotel bar for hours. She'd felt overwhelmed then, too, but it'd been almost wonderful to feel so aware of someone. Now she knew it wasn't wonderful, and Zayed Fehr wasn't wonderful. He'd use whatever he had to get what he wanted. It was his way. And she despised him for it.

"Go away," Rou choked, stumbling to her feet. "Please. Please, Sheikh Fehr. Just go away and leave me alone." She was trembling from head to foot, knew she'd lost all reason, knew she'd lost all control.

This was what she'd wanted to avoid. This was why she'd left Vancouver. Zayed Fehr threatened her. He shattered her control. He made her feel like a panicked girl instead of the scientist she was, and she couldn't allow it. She wasn't that strong. Smart, yes; successful, yes; strong? No. No. Only on paper. Only on the surface.

Her gaze darted around the ballroom as she planned her escape. If she skirted the dance floor, cut through the tables in the corner, moved behind the ice sculpture, she'd reach the doors on the side that led to the entry hall with the cloakroom.

Zayed placed a restraining hand over hers, preventing her from leaving. "Calm yourself, Dr. Tornell...."

"I can't! You won't let me. You won't leave me alone."

"I'm not trying to hurt you, Dr. Tornell. I need you. I need..."

Rou didn't hear the rest. She was suddenly enveloped in a giant hug. "Rou, you naughty thing, where have you been? I've been looking all over for you!"

Georgina's breathless voice penetrated Rou's panic-fogged brain.

Gratefully she hugged Georgina back. Georgina. The wedding. Vienna. Everything was fine. Everything would be fine.

"You look beautiful," Rou whispered unsteadily, giving Georgina a hard squeeze. "I've never seen a happier bride."

"All thanks to you," Georgina whispered. "You said there were no princes, but you found one for me!"

Georgina stepped back, and Ralf leaned down and dropped a kiss on Rou's cheek. "I will always be in your debt, Dr. Tornell."

And then Ralf and Georgina were turning their attention to Zayed, heartily welcoming him, and thanking him for coming.

"It is my pleasure," Zayed answered smoothly, "and I offer you my family's warmest congratulations on your marriage."

"Thank you," Ralf replied. "But tell us, have you news of Sharif? We've only just heard. It was on the television earlier."

"Was it?" Zayed answered. "I didn't think they were going to go public for another few days."

Ralf and Georgina exchanged swift glances. "Is it true that there's no sign of the plane? That it just totally disappeared from the radar?" Ralf persisted.

Zayed nodded.

"And Jesslyn?" Georgina asked. "Is she... Was she...?"

"She wasn't with him, no. Nor the children, thank God." Zayed's expression shifted, hardened. "Although they were all supposed to be together."

"I can't believe it," Ralf said, more to himself than the others. "Sharif is so….so…Sharif."

Zayed inclined his head, and Ralf quickly recovered and reached out to clasp Zayed's shoulder. "We are praying for him, and all of you. We must not lose hope. And if there is anything we can do, any way we can aid the search, or help the queen, you only need to say the word."

The wedding couple moved on.

Rou was silent for a moment after Georgina and Ralf walked away, but then she turned to Zayed, her expression fierce. "What's happened to Sharif?"

"I've told you—"

"You haven't."

"He's missing. His plane disappeared ten days ago. But I told you—"

"No, you didn't tell me." Her voice cracked. "You definitely didn't tell me. You said throne, Sarq, kingdom. You didn't say Sharif. You didn't say he was missing. You didn't. And you should have."

"Why?"

"Why?" Her eyes shimmered with tears. "He's my hero. I adore him, and I'd do anything, absolutely anything, for him."

CHAPTER THREE

THEY'D agreed they'd meet in the morning, at nine in his hotel lobby.

They were to start afresh.

At least that's what she'd told Zayed. But Rou spent a sleepless night in her hotel bed, tossing and turning with the weight of her thoughts and the enormity of her dread.

She adored Sharif. She feared Zayed.

She'd promised to help Zayed but only because of Sharif.

If she hadn't been the recipient of the Fehr scholarship at Cambridge. If she hadn't been mentored by Sharif for six of her eight years at university. If she hadn't admired Sharif so terribly, maybe she could walk away from Zayed now, but she had been a Fehr scholar, and Sharif had been her mentor, and she did think of him as the older brother she never had.

Sharif was missing. And Sarq was in turmoil.

Of course she'd help Zayed. How could she not? But she'd limit the time she spent with him and would monitor his proximity. There was no reason she couldn't work with him over the phone, or via e-mail and fax. She'd just sit down with him in the morning, get the paperwork started and then complete the rest from a safe and sane distance.

The key thing was getting Sharif found, and Zayed back to Sarq where he could assume leadership until his brother returned.

Because Sharif would be found. Sharif would return—alive. It had to be. There was no other possibility. Not for his wife, Jesslyn, or his four children, or his country. Sharif was too well loved.

Zayed, on the other hand, was not as well loved. Rou knew from the little Sharif had said that Zayed, the middle brother, was the family black sheep, and had been for much of Sharif's life, a thorn in his side.

Just as he was fast becoming a thorn in hers.

The next morning, Zayed's bodyguards preceded him out of the hotel elevator and then took up positions as Zayed crossed the expansive marble lobby floor in search of Rou.

After a moment he spotted her, seated at a low table across the lobby, dressed in a sober gray skirt and jacket.

This morning her hair was drawn tightly back from her face in a severe knot at her nape, her thin body angled away from the table as she hunched over her computer leaving just her legs exposed. And they were, he noted with some surprise, endless legs. Long, shapely legs. Truly remarkable legs.

Zayed slowed his pace, frankly admiring the long legs that curved to the side of the gold chair, low kitten heels, her skirt a demure hem length, her sheer stockings revealing pale skin beneath.

Then, as if on cue, she with the long legs and severe blond chignon turned her head and looked directly at him.

He exhaled.

And she was back to being plain, uptight Dr. Tornell. In all fairness, Rou Tornell wasn't greyhound ugly, but she wasn't beautiful. She couldn't even be called pretty. This morning she wore glasses, dark tortoiseshell glasses that looked stark against her pale skin, perching too large on her small, straight nose. Her mouth was thin. Her chin strong.

Zayed, so rarely amused by anything, nearly smiled now. Little Miss Muffet. That's what she was. And he was the spider.

The only thing he didn't know as he sat down across from her was how such a prim and proper Miss Muffet ended up with legs of sin?

Rou noticed Zayed's peculiar expression as he took a seat in the upholstered chair across from hers. "Everything all right?" she asked.

"I haven't heard anything new," he answered, "if that's what you mean."

She nodded once. It was what she'd meant and Zayed, satisfied, opened his briefcase and pulled out folders, notebooks, handouts.

He slid one of the stapled handouts toward her.

"I've already filled out your client profile, including family background and medical history."

She glanced at the packet in front of her. They were her own confidential client forms. "These are my forms," she said, clearly surprised.

"I told you, I did my research."

"But where did you get these?"

Zayed shook his head, reading her like a book. "It wasn't your assistant. I just did some legwork."

Rou's eyebrows shot up. "Don't cover for Jamie—"

"It was Pippa, if you must know. I phoned her and she was happy to send me copies of her paperwork. My secretary made me clean copies." But Zayed was already moving on. "This is the Myers-Briggs personality test you use. I've completed it, as well, although I could have told you what I am—I've been tested before—but I was certain you'd want the proof in front of you."

"You've left me very little to do," she protested, although her tone indicated she was only half joking.

"Not at all. Now comes the important part. You find her for me. That is what all these forms lead to, isn't it? Mate selection?"

Mate selection, Rou echoed silently.

Those were her words, from her own material, but it sounded so dry, so businesslike coming from him. She looked up at him, and as her gaze met his, her heart did a crazy lurch, a disturbing feeling that made her feel off-kilter.

Rou didn't appreciate the way her pulse had begun to race.

It hadn't raced this way in years, either. It'd been so long since she'd felt this desperate giddiness, this awful breathlessness. It'd been, well, since Lady Pippa's wedding, when she'd allowed herself to be charmed by Zayed.

Only Zayed hadn't been charmed. He'd found her dull and ridiculous, and he'd said so to Sharif.

You can't let him do this to you again, she admonished herself severely. You're not attracted to him, and it's not emotion making you feel this way, either. It's down to hormones and chemicals, silly involuntary chemicals like dopamine and adrenaline. You don't even like him. You resent him. You despise him. And you only respond this way because he makes you nervous, he makes you afraid.

And it was true. Every time she was around him, her heart raced, and her stomach got this sick, nauseous feel. As if she were on a rocking boat. Or a plane dancing in a turbulent wake.

Or trapped in the backseat of a car with her parents screaming.

Zayed's hand was suddenly at her elbow. "Are you going to faint?" he asked.

"No." She pulled forcefully from his grasp. "I'm perfectly fine."

"You're looking very pale."

"I was born pale," she answered fiercely, seeing from his expression that he didn't appear convinced. "Now, can we focus on the business at hand? You need a wife, if I recall, and you've asked me to help find her for you."

They turned their attention to the paperwork then, and his profile. For the next hour she asked questions and he answered. They were just starting their second hour of work when his phone rang. He'd ignored earlier calls but seeing the number he answered this one.

He said just a few words and then nothing else. Instead he listened. And Rou sat, notepad on her lap, and watched his face.

The color left his face. His expression changed, the life in his eyes fading. By the time he hung up, he looked dead.

"They've found the plane," he said, slowly sliding the phone into his coat pocket. "Or they think it's the plane. The fire made identifying the machine impossible but they have recovered the black box. We should know more soon."

She held his gaze, unable to speak.

"I have to return to Sarq. I'm needed. You'll go with me. We can finish this en route."

She nodded when she should have protested. She was supposed to be limiting her contact with him, putting space between them instead of close proximity, but after news like this, there was no way she'd deny her help now.

Ninety minutes after the call they were airborne in Zayed's personal jet.

It crossed Rou's mind as the jet cut through the sky in a steep ascent that flying was not safe. Being alone with Zayed Fehr wasn't safe. And accompanying him to his desert kingdom definitely could be the most dangerous thing of all.

But then life wasn't safe.

And just like that, Sharif's voice was in her head. *Your thoughts become your future.*

Yes. He was right, of course. Right as always. He'd been the first one to make her understand that emotions weren't always right, or accurate. He'd explained to her that the most recent psychology findings revealed a clear connection between thoughts and feelings. Between thoughts and emotions.

If you thought happy thoughts, you felt happier.

If you thought the world was good, you'd see the world as good.

It was such a revelation for a girl who'd known too many years of unhappiness.

Her life, her happiness, didn't hinge on others. She could choose to be happy even if the world was in the midst of misery.

She looked away from the window and discovered Zayed watching her, his amazing features still perfect and yet his eyes were dark. Tortured.

"Have you really never been in love?" she blurted, surprising herself with the question.

He took a long time to answer, which was unlike him as he always had a ready response. "No," he finally said, "but I'm not without feeling. I have deep ties to my family, particularly my older brother."

She could see his bio sheet in her mind, and the facts describing his family. Father—deceased. Mother—

still living. Older brother—40, married, father of four. Younger brother—33, married, wife expecting. Younger sisters—deceased.

Much of his family was a mystery, but she did know about his sisters. It was why Sharif founded the scholarship at Cambridge. He'd started the scholarship in their memory. "Your sisters," she said to Zayed now, "were you close to them?"

"Very."

She waited for him to say more but he didn't. "They died together, didn't they?" she asked, hoping he'd elaborate.

"Car accident in Greece. They were young, early twenties." His voice betrayed no emotion, but she saw the small muscle tighten in his jaw and his right hand curled into a fist, fingers clenching air.

"Their deaths were hard for the family?" she persisted.

He shot her a hard look. "How is this relevant?"

"It's part of you, part of your family...."

"I'm not looking for a love match, Dr. Tornell. I'm looking for a wife. She doesn't have to understand my every dark secret. She'll never be my soul mate."

Rou's gaze lifted from his fist to his face. His handsome features were utterly expressionless and yet those tightly bunched fingers gave him away. "You don't want a soul mate?"

"No. I just want a practical relationship. One that works."

She looked at him levelly. "Not many women will find your idea of marriage palatable."

"I'm sure there are practical women out there."

She arched her eyebrows but said nothing more as she scribbled in the margins of his notes that yes, his sisters' deaths had profoundly impacted him. He feared love because he feared loss.

"Did you ever want to be king?" she asked, wondering what it'd be like to lose three of your four siblings. She'd been an only child, couldn't imagine having a brother or sister to love, although she'd wanted one desperately. It was what she'd asked Santa Claus to bring her for years until her mother finally told her that Santa wasn't real. He was just a fat old man in a red cloth suit.

"No. It wasn't part of my ambition or my life plan." He hesitated. "But things change, and the situation is what it is now, and I cannot let my brother down. I must be there for him so that when he returns..." He didn't finish the thought.

"Do you think he will be found alive?"

"Yes."

Rou felt a wave of sympathy for him. He had to be aware that after ten days Sharif might not be found, or if he was, he might not be alive. "What if he's not?"

"Sharif isn't dead."

She nodded once, realizing that she and Zayed had at least this in common: both refused to believe that Sharif was dead. They wouldn't, not without firm proof, not without a body.

She shivered inwardly at the thought, and quickly changed the direction of her thoughts. "Would you like to work? Or do you need some time?"

"No, let's work. I need to work."

She nodded again and reached for her briefcase, which she'd slid beneath her leather seat. Work had always been her salvation. Work would help both of them now.

The flight attendant arrived and unhooked the table attached to the wall, setting it up between Zayed and Rou's club chairs, and offered to serve them lunch.

Zayed looked at her. "We have a fully stocked kitchen with a chef on board."

"Just tea," she answered. "I don't think I could eat a bite right now."

"I feel the same way," he answered. "One tea, one coffee," he instructed the flight attendant and she disappeared to prepare their beverages.

Rou had found the paperwork she wanted, and with pen in hand she looked at Zayed. He was tall and powerfully built and blessed with almost godlike beauty, and yet there was pain in his eyes, in the press of his beautiful, sensual mouth, and she drew a deep breath.

She was not immune to him. But then, she'd never been immune to him, which was incredibly foolish as he was handsome and wealthy and oozed sensuality, while she was at best a smart little church mouse.

Rou knew her strengths and her weaknesses, and while she was brainy, she was far from beautiful.

Perhaps if she'd been blessed with more curves she might have felt more sexually confident, but she'd inherited her mother's extreme slimness, which meant she was rather narrow hipped and disappointingly small on top.

No, men like Zayed Fehr never noticed women like her. They wanted sirens—voluptuous beauties with thick glossy hair, full lips and come-hither eyes.

Rou wouldn't know a come-hither expression if it smacked her in the face.

But on the positive side, it was good that Zayed was oblivious to her as a woman. She couldn't have handled his attention otherwise. As it was, he wreaked havoc on her emotions and her control, making her jumpy and nervous. Making her heart skitter and race and her hands shake.

They were shaking now and she tried to hide her anxiety by shuffling the paperwork until she found the page she needed. "We're to the part where I ask you to describe your ideal woman," she said coolly, gratified by the firm tone of her voice. "Can you give me five adjectives that would describe her?"

He thought for a moment. "Intelligent. Accomplished. Successful." He thought another moment. "Confident, loyal. And preferably beautiful." He hesitated. "But that's six, isn't it?"

"It's okay. Six is good, too." Of course he'd ask for beauty. All men did. And Zayed Fehr was famous for squiring the world's most beautiful women about town. "So a model, maybe?"

"No. Definitely not a model. Or an actress. Nothing like that."

Rou lifted her head in surprise. "Really?"

He didn't seem to register her surprise as he added to his description of his ideal woman. "Most important is intelligence. I admire women who are accomplished. And successful. But she must be kind. A woman that's compassionate. Maybe a teacher or a nurse."

Rou checked her frown. A teacher or a nurse? "Like Sharif's wife? Jesslyn was a teacher, too."

He nodded. "Khalid's wife is very kind, too. They're always thinking of others. I like that, respect that."

"Right." She scribbled a few more words onto the form, although she couldn't help thinking that he was steering her in a very different direction than she might have gone on her own. But this was why they went through the process. "What about sense of humor? Sense of adventure? Introvert? Extrovert? Do you see yourself doing a lot of entertaining? Should she be comfortable as a hostess? Will she need to have public speaking skills? Are you expecting her to be a leader in fashion, or be artistic?"

"It depends on the woman. Oh, and she needs to be strong."

"*Strong?*"

"Mentally…emotionally. I don't want a subservient woman. She must be able to hold her own with me, as well as my family. It can be an intimidating family and although Sarq is more modern than many

of our neighbors, it is still a Middle Eastern kingdom and quite different from our Western friends
and allies."

Rou's pen hovered in midair. He was describing a
woman she would never have picked for him. She would
have thought he'd want a gorgeous bimbo, or a sultry
beauty who'd make him look good in public. But beauty
was sixth on his wish list. Intelligence was number one.
Interesting, but puzzling, which made her realize she
knew far less about Zayed than she'd thought.

The flight attendant returned with a tray holding
their cups and her pot of tea, along with a plate of light
biscuits and fruit and cheese.

Rou found herself reaching for a dark red grape and
then a small wedge of cheese and realized she hadn't
eaten since last night. She'd been so nervous this
morning she'd only drunk coffee. A little food was
good. A little food now would go a long way.

She glanced up and saw Zayed studying her again,
his brow furrowed. She reached for the linen serviette
and brushed at her mouth. "What's wrong? Do I have
something on my face?"

"No. It's good to see you eat. You're so very thin—"

"My mother was thin," she interrupted, "Unfortunately I inherited her fast metabolism instead of her
stunning cheekbones." Rou smiled at her own joke but
Zayed didn't smile back.

"I suspect you don't eat enough."

"Sharif used to say the same thing. But I have this
terribly sensitive stomach. When I'm nervous, or

anxious, I can't eat anything. My throat just closes up and tea is about all I can manage."

His golden gaze had darkened at the mention of Sharif's name. "You knew my brother well?"

Rou glanced down at her lap where she spread the linen cloth flat. "I think you know I earned the Fehr scholarship at Cambridge. It's what helped me pay for all my graduate studies."

"And that's why you're so devoted to Sharif?"

She felt herself blush. "No. But Sharif became a friend as well as a mentor during my years at Cambridge. It wasn't until after I'd earned my advance degrees that I realized he helped me because of his sisters."

"How did he help?" Zayed persisted.

"He offered advice and wisdom. He listened to my goals. He made introductions when he could." She looked at Zayed, saw the skepticism in his expression and shrugged. "I know it sounds strange. Your brother is a powerful man, a very wealthy man, but he's also a compassionate man, and I think in his own way, he needed me as much as I needed him."

"Sharif needs no one. He's the rock of the family. Invincible."

Rou wrinkled her brow. "You think so?"

"From birth he's been groomed to lead. From the start he's known what is expected of him and he's done it, without complaint."

"But that doesn't mean he hasn't felt loss, or pain. Or worry, or doubt."

"You're not describing my brother—"

"And you just don't want to see your brother as a man, and vulnerable."

"Sharif isn't vulnerable. He's never been vulnerable, and he's going to be found. He'll be back in Sarq, running the country again in no time."

Rou studied him curiously. "If you really believe that, then why go to all the trouble of finding a proper wife and getting married? Why not just wait for his return?"

"I can't." His tone was curt, his frustration evident. "Sarq law requires a present king, therefore I must assume the throne, but I can't without a bride."

She was silent a moment, digesting this, as well as wondering how to best word what she wanted to say next. "Sheikh Fehr, I have to be honest. If you want a woman to marry you so you can assume the throne, then that's one thing. But if you want a woman who is your life partner, that's entirely different."

"The woman needs to be one and the same. I need a bride, and I want a successful marriage. Surely you have someone in your system who would be open to a short courtship? Someone not opposed to, say, an arranged marriage? Someone who would benefit from my position, and wealth? Someone who could contribute to our lives here…?"

She knew the answer. It was no. None of the women she'd met and represented would want to be whisked here, married within days, and then left here for the next twenty-some years. For most modern women it'd be a horrific prospect. "Forgive me, but Sarq is in the middle of nowhere."

"Yes."

"You're isolated."

"And…?"

"Do you intend to remain here permanently, then? Or will you live part-time in Monte Carlo? I know you have a home there."

"As king I have to live where my people live."

"And your new bride?"

He gave her a look that indicated she might have lost her mind. "She'd live with me, of course."

She ran a hand over her eyes, already exhausted. This was impossible. He had to realize that, didn't he? Wonderful, successful, intelligent, confident, strong women didn't just run to the Middle East and marry a sheikh and stay there, buried in the desert. It was one thing if a woman was desperate, or had no choice, but the woman he described as his ideal wife would have a choice, and she wouldn't find his life as a desert king appealing. "I know you don't want to hear this, but you're describing an arranged marriage, and if you want an arranged marriage, you're better off with a woman from your own culture—"

"No."

"—who could embrace the concept of arranged marriage," she continued as though he'd never spoken. "Western women *won't*."

"Why not?"

"You know the answer to this. You've only dated

Western women for years. Women in the West don't want to get married because they have to, or because he has to. They want to marry because they're desired and loved and cherished."

His strong, black brows flattened, emphasizing the lines of his high, hard cheekbones and straight nose. "But I would respect and cherish my wife."

She noted he said respect and cherish, not love and cherish but she didn't comment on that. "It takes time for a woman to know that, as well as examples. Proof. That's why men court women. They're showing women how they'd be treated…what they can expect. It's a wooing, and you're not leaving time for that."

"I'll do it after the ceremony. Just let her know it will happen."

"After the ceremony?" She gave him her sternest look. "And now one last question. It's sensitive since I know we're coming from two different cultures, but I need to know about the political and social rights of women. Are women considered equals in Sarq? Are there laws to protect them? What rights do women have?"

"Women do not have all the rights of men—yet. But that is something Sharif has been working to change, and I will make this a priority, as well."

"So what if a woman—your woman—breaks the law? What would happen to her?"

"I'd protect her."

"But could you?" Rou leaned forward, urgency in her voice. "Could you truly?"

"Do you doubt my word?"

"No, I don't doubt your word. I just want what's best for your future wife—"

"And you think I don't?" he interrupted almost violently, his features dark, his expression fierce.

She stared up at him in stunned silence. She'd never seen him like this, never heard this anger in his voice before, either. "No," she stuttered.

"Good. Consider the subject closed." He rose from the table and walked away, disappearing into a cabin at the back of the plane.

The back cabin of the jet had been designed as a small, snug and yet exceptionally comfortable bedroom. Zayed sat heavily on the edge of the low bed and covered his face with his hands.

He rarely lost his temper. He hated that he'd lost it now. But her questions…those questions…

She didn't understand. She'd never understand. No one had ever understood.

He wasn't like the rest of his family. He was different. Cursed. And yet once, he and his brothers had all been the same, all raised the same. Arab princes, beloved sons of the desert, children of fortune.

And although Zayed was the middle of the three princes, and the second-eldest of five, he'd been his father's favorite and he knew it. He'd never wondered why he was the favorite, either, he'd just accepted it, just as he accepted his good fortune. Just as he'd accepted that he was destined for greatness, and great things. In the beginning it was so clear that fate had favored him, so obvious he would live a blessed life.

But he'd been wrong.

It wasn't a blessed life. It was cursed. *He* was cursed.

And so he took himself away from the desert and his family, away from the people who might be hurt by his curse and turned to the pleasures of the world, only there was no pleasure when one was cursed.

Would he protect his wife?

He would try with all his heart and soul and might. But would it be enough?

If he didn't love her, and she didn't love him, would the marriage somehow escape the curse?

He didn't know, but he could only hope.

CHAPTER FOUR

Rou watched the closed door of the plane cabin with her heart in her mouth. She didn't exactly know what she said that had upset Zayed—something about protecting his wife—but clearly she'd offended him. She wanted to apologize, or at least try to set things right. They had so much to do. Tension wouldn't help.

The flight attendant appeared after fifteen minutes to refresh her tea, and then another fifteen minutes later she returned to remove the dishes and take down the table.

"We'll be landing in about fifty minutes," she said, smiling at Rou. "Is there anything else I could get you?"

Rou shook her head and thanked her.

Just when Rou thought Zayed would never return, and the pilot had announced they would soon begin their final descent, Zayed arrived, and took his seat across from her, his expression blank, revealing nothing.

"I'm sorry," she said awkwardly.

"You did nothing wrong," he answered emotionlessly.

She didn't feel any better, though, and her eyebrows tugged together. "I tend to be very blunt."

"I prefer honesty."

"And I ask a lot of questions."

"It's your job."

Right. Rou exhaled slowly, heavily, definitely not feeling any better.

Zayed gazed fixedly outside the window and Rou, biting the inside of her lip, did the same, and they didn't speak again until they were on the ground.

Their jet ended up landing at the Sarq air force airport, and it was only once the plane's wheels touched down that Zayed explained this wasn't where the Fehr family usually landed, as they had their own royal airport. But with Sharif's accident, Zayed's plane had been given a military escort to ensure his safe arrival. The country couldn't lose two kings, not in a fortnight.

Heavy security awaited them as they deplaned. Armed soldiers, as well as undercover security in dark suits, lined the tarmac.

Rou sucked in a breath as she stepped from the plane into the late-afternoon sun. Heat rose from the black tarmac in scorching waves. It might be late October but the temperature hovered in the nineties and her gray wool suit felt suffocating now.

"It's hot," she murmured when Zayed turned to look at her where she still stood on the stairs.

"It's actually cooler than it was just weeks ago." He reached out a hand to her.

Rou glanced at his hand and then up into his face. He was still distant, still reserved. She told herself she should be pleased by the distance—she couldn't encourage intimacy of any sort—but she worried about him now, and she didn't want to do that, either.

Reluctantly she put her hand in his, and nearly jumped at the hot, tingly sensation of his skin against hers. It took all her concentration to make it down the steep stairs without falling.

Distance was good, she told herself, gripping her briefcase in the other hand. Distance was necessary.

On the tarmac Zayed gestured to her briefcase. "Leave that. Someone will bring it."

"But it's my computer and files. I need it."

"Security must check all bags and luggage before anything is permitted to enter the palace grounds."

"Oh. Okay." She handed him the briefcase. "But I will get it back as soon as possible?"

"As soon as possible," he promised before handing the briefcase to one of the security detail waiting at the bottom of the stairs.

The drive to the palace in the armored car with the bulletproof glass was quiet, but it wasn't a comfortable silence. They were sitting side by side on the soft leather seat and the seat had too much give and Rou felt as though she was sitting far too close to Zayed, but there was really nowhere else to go. He was big, and his shoulders broad, and his legs—long and muscular—crowded her own.

She could feel him even though he wasn't touching her, and the more aware of him she was, the warmer she became, and the warmer she became, the faster her heart beat.

Why did she have to do this around him? Why couldn't she treat him like any other man? Why did she care that she felt so dowdy and gawky and dull?

Because a little part of you likes him, a small voice answered inside her.

A little part of you wants him to like you back.

Ridiculous! she silently flashed, cutting off the little voice. He's shallow and unkind, selfish and untrustworthy. Why would I like him?

But when Zayed's head suddenly turned and he fixed his gold gaze on her, her stomach flipped and her chest grew tight and she drew a quick, panicked breath, terribly dizzy.

This was such a bad idea coming here with him....

"This is Isi," he said, nodding to the buildings and landscape beyond the window, "Sarq's capital city."

Grateful for the distraction, she turned her head to have a better look at the city that gleamed beneath the hard glaze of sunlight. So many of the buildings appeared new, and fountains and palm trees lined the wide, elegant boulevards. Whereas there were robed women on the streets, there were also a surprising number in fashionable Western dress.

Their caravan of armored Mercedes limousines turned down a long drive bordered by towering stuccoed walls covered in lush purple-and-pink bougainvillea, while soaring palm trees dotted the drive with puddles of sunshine and shadows.

The cars stopped as massive wood-and-iron gates, gates that had to be easily ten feet tall or more, swung slowly open and then they were passing through the gates and around more walls until Rou got a glimpse of a sprawling pink building marked by fanciful domes and arches.

"The palace," Zayed said gruffly.

She glanced at him, saw the mixture of pride and pain in his face and turned back to the view of the elaborate compound.

The entrance, marked by exquisite carved columns and a gold-painted dome, was suddenly filled with white-robed staff. They lined the entrance, bowing, welcoming Zayed home.

A prince's welcome.

Security opened the car door and stepped back so that Zayed could exit. She'd expected him to move on toward his staff, but once again he turned to her first, helping her from the car and waiting for her to adjust her suit skirt and jacket before they moved forward.

Once she was ready, they walked inside, between the silent, bowing staff, and through the carved columns into the cool, serene interior.

Whereas the exterior of the palace was pale pink like a delicate flower, the interior walls were painted white and the ceiling a mosaic of gold and blue. Columned hallways led in every direction and priceless sculpture filled the airy halls. It was spectacular, and Rou, who had visited her share of palaces, had never seen anything so wonderful, or so exotic. This was like something from *Arabian Nights*, or a Hollywood film set.

"It's amazing," she breathed, as Zayed turned to her after greeting key staff. "This is where you grew up?"

His lips curved ruefully, the first smile since the phone call earlier that morning in Vienna, and something in his smile made her heart turn over. His smile hinted at the boy he'd once been, a boy she suspected he rarely acknowledged. "This is home," he admitted.

She felt another quick stab of feeling, a strange protective emotion she didn't understand. "You are a prince, aren't you?"

His smile slowly faded. "You wouldn't know it from the way I behaved. Is that what you're saying?"

"No! Not at all." She put an impulsive hand on his sleeve, shocked that he so misread her, but when Zayed glanced down at her hand, she realized she'd committed a faux pas. Commoners probably weren't allowed to touch the royal family.

Embarrassed and uncomfortable she pulled her hand away, clenched it into a fist and hid it behind her back. "I should get to work. Just show me to a desk and I'll wait for my computer."

Zayed turned to one of his staff, spoke in a language she didn't understand and then turned back to her. "Arrangements have been made for you to use one of our family suites."

He saw her expression and added, "Don't worry. It's no longer in use and it has good light, plenty of space where you can work and access to a small private garden should you need some fresh air."

The servant in the white robe stepped forward. "If you will come with me, my lady," he said formally, bowing to her.

The room Rou was given wasn't merely a room, but an entire suite of rooms, one of those elegant compounds down a columned, arched corridor. Late, lingering sunlight poured through the arched glass doors, flooding the sunken living room with light, turning the silk pillows on the couch into glowing gems. A massive arrangement of fragrant coral-hued roses dominated the low table in the middle of the room and scented the room with spicy perfume.

A young robed woman appeared under one of the arches. "Welcome," she said shyly with a bow. "I am Manar, and I am to make you comfortable. I will be here with you as long as you are here."

"Thank you, Manar. That is very kind of you, but I don't really need anything. Just my computer so I can start working."

"It is here," Manar answered with a gesture toward a small antique desk in the corner of the room. The desk had been angled to provide a view of the garden wall, and her briefcase sat on top of the desk.

"Wonderful." She pushed up her suit's wool sleeves and approached the desk. "I think I'm set then."

Manar looked at her doubtfully as Rou took a seat at the desk. "You do not wish to bathe or change?"

Rou was already pulling out her computer and preparing to set it up. "Hmm?" she asked, realizing Manar was waiting for a response.

"You do not wish to change into something more comfortable for work?"

Rou shook her head briskly, determined to do what she needed to do so she could leave as soon as possible. "No. I'm fine. But thank you." And then she was turning her computer on and all thoughts were on the work before her.

Alone in the living room, she adjusted the reading light on the desk, and stacked her notebooks next to her computer, and prepared to enter the information she'd learned this morning and during the flight. But her fingers wouldn't obey. She balked at completing the online spreadsheets.

It just seemed wrong to do this.

It seemed wrong to be helping Zayed find a wife this way. Her gut said that Zayed needed a love marriage, not an arranged marriage. Her gut said he was a man with deeper feelings than he let on. But he wasn't asking for her intuition, he wanted her skills to pair him with a suitable woman. At least, if there was sufficient time.

Just input the rest of the profile, she told herself. *Do what he's hired you to do.*

But still she couldn't type. Her fingers wouldn't respond. Her mind wouldn't respond.

When she closed her eyes in frustration all she saw was Zayed, and not just his beautiful profile but his tortured expression, and she could hear his anger and she knew there was something else bothering him, something else eating at him. Only what?

Yet her obsession with Zayed was beginning to annoy her. She was here to work. This was business, pure and simple. So why then was she so conflicted?

Why was she acting so out of character? Rou never let herself dwell on emotions. She didn't cater to them or acknowledge them and certainly didn't give in to them. Emotions were the enemy of the scientist. Thoughts, logic, reason—those were the basis for all scientific theory.

She just needed to focus on science now. Needed to clear her head and remember what was important, what mattered.

Theory. Study. Proof.

And yet, and yet…there were feelings inside her that wouldn't be stifled. Feelings that were disturbingly intense, and distractingly real, and they ached in her now, and it was a physical ache, a heartache. And it was all because of him. Zayed Fehr.

Rou exhaled and, resting her elbows on the desk, she covered her face with her hands.

She still had feelings for him. That's why she still responded to him. That's why she wanted him to like her, admire her. *Foolish, foolish Rou,* she thought. *So book smart and so people stupid.*

She sat for a long moment, face hidden, heart thudding, stomach knotted with misery.

And then the survival instinct kicked in. She knew what she had to do. She had to get him matched and married and she had to get out of here. Soon. Because

Zayed Fehr was dangerous. If she wasn't careful, he'd take that too-warm, too-tender spot in her heart and rip it wide-open.

Lavender shadows dappled the courtyard outside her window by the time Rou finished inputting her information. It had taken her far longer than usual to complete the profile, but at last it was done and now the computer program she'd designed would match him with suitable candidates.

She waited while the computer sorted and then put together a list of possibilities. The program gave her thirty. Not bad.

Rou was still reading through the profiles when Manar returned. "His Highness would like to see you. Are you able to receive guests now?"

"Yes, of course," Rou answered, rising, even as she reached up to touch her hair, thinking only now that perhaps she should have run a comb through it, or freshened herself a little.

But Zayed arrived immediately, and she remained on her feet as he entered the suite.

"I have your first candidates," she said nervously. "I can print off the profiles and you can study them when you have time, or we could go through them now—"

"It is his plane." Zayed's voice was low, rough. "It doesn't appear there were any survivors."

Rou slowly sat back down in her chair. *"No."*

"The bodies were charred, nearly unrecognizable…." He came to a stop, arms at his sides, and for the first time there was real despair on his face, in his voice. "They have to run tests. They've asked for dental records."

Rou stared at him in mute horror. So it'd come to this. The jet. The remains of the bodies. Sharif's body. Her mind shuddered in grief, in horror. "His wife," she whispered.

"Beside herself."

She bit down into her lower lip, biting hard to keep tears from welling in her eyes.

"I'm sorry," he added roughly.

He was sorry? He was apologizing to *her*? Rou's eyes filled with tears. Her chest burned with livid emotion, emotion she hadn't felt in years. "I'm sorry," she choked, "I'm so sorry for all of you—"

"I have to make this right."

"Yes, of course."

"I will make it right." He walked toward her, crossing the sunken floor, and it wasn't until he stepped into the light that she realized he was wearing a white robe. She'd never seen him in traditional Sarq dress. "But there isn't a lot of time. The coronation is in forty-eight hours."

She looked from the white robe up to his bronze profile. He was recently shaven and his cheekbones jutted high and hard against his skin. "So soon?"

"Can you find me a queen in forty-eight hours?"

Her gaze held his. This wasn't a moment of celebration, it was a tragedy, a travesty. The whole country would be mourning. Sharif's family would be mourning. "Perhaps we can find you prospects—"

"No, not prospects. A bride. I told you, I have to be married. There must be an actual ceremony."

"But how does anyone expect you to marry and become king within two days of learning that your brother is dead?"

He stopped in the middle of the sunken living room, stared down at the bowl of lush, lavish roses. "Kings are not like other men. They sacrifice for the good of their country."

He leaned down to snap a blossom from the stem and carried it to his nose. "These roses were planted after my sisters died. Sharif created the memorial garden for my parents and when the twelve rose-bushes arrived, he dug each of the twelve holes, planting the roses personally." Zayed lifted his head, looked at Rou. "I must honor my brother. I must serve my country. I must make the transition of power as smooth, as easy as possible. It is the least I can do."

With the rose still cupped in his palm, Zayed turned to leave, but he paused on the steps. "I will have a printer brought to you and if you could please print off the profiles and bring them with you, we will discuss them later."

"You don't wish to look at them now?"

"I have to speak with Khalid. I've an emergency cabinet meeting. The press—" He broke off, jaw grinding hard, eyes glittering with unspeakable sorrow. "But I want to see them. I will meet you later."

"Of course. Anytime."

He nodded, staring blindly across the room. Silence stretched. Finally he spoke, his voice low and hoarse. "I thought he'd survive. I was sure he'd survive. I was sure…"

She swallowed around the knot filling her throat. "Maybe he did."

Zayed shot her a sharp look. "You're just as bad as I am."

"Until they give you proof…?"

He shook his head, a short savage shake. "I clung to hope before. I won't do it now. The disappointment is too severe." He drew a breath, his chest rising, and then exhaled hard. "I'll meet you for a late dinner. We'll talk then. Bring the profiles."

"Okay."

And then he was gone.

For a moment she sat frozen in place, her mind reeling, her emotions chaotic. Sharif…Zayed… Sarq…

Her eyes burned and her throat felt raw and she didn't know how long she sat there, but finally, the sound of footsteps in the hall roused her, and she turned as Manar appeared. "Your printer has arrived," she said in her soft voice.

Rou had forgotten all about the printer, and wasn't sure Zayed would even remember such a small un-important detail when he had so much on his mind. But he had.

The printer wasn't the only equipment that arrived.

Zayed had also sent along a copier, another desk and reams of paper. Rou stood aside as the efficient staff assembled an office for her right before her eyes, creating an L-shaped work area for her, and then taping down extension cords onto the stone floor before disappearing.

She could still hear their retreating footsteps when she numbly sat down to print off the first ten profiles, and then she printed the next ten, just in case.

She worked without thinking, without feeling, worked just to stay busy. As she compiled the profiles as they emerged from the printer, her thoughts drifted to a former client, a difficult client. He was an American high-tech billionaire, and he believed first impressions were everything. He hated the first sixty head shots of the first sixty profiles she'd presented—no, no, no—but fell in love with sixty-one. He ended up marrying her and today they had three small children.

With her prep work complete, Rou still had several hours to fill. She took a nap, and then a long bath and after washing her hair she dressed again in the same gray suit she'd worn earlier. She didn't have many choices, having brought only her small Vienna suitcase with her, but it was a good suit, she told herself, and Zayed wouldn't care. Zayed wouldn't even notice what she wore, anyway. To Zayed she was just a thing, an object, like the printer or copier now sitting on the desk.

After blow-drying her hair, Rou twisted it into another simple knot, and then slipped back on the same heels she'd worn in the morning. She applied no makeup; she never wore makeup, and rarely wore jewelry. She'd always prided herself on being sensible and practical, although a little part of her would have loved once—just once—to have been thought beautiful. To have maybe dazzled.

Manar arrived promptly at nine, bowed and asked Rou to come with her. Rou gathered her leather portfolio with the stack of profiles and followed Manar from her suite to a distant wing in the palace.

She was led to a small dining room softly lit by candles on the low table and in the oversize gold chandelier hanging above the table. Large, plump cushions in shades of blue were scattered on the floor around the table and the walls were covered in dark, carved screens. Above the chandelier the ceiling was domed and a dark midnight blue inlaid with bars of gold.

Manar bowed and left her, and Rou wandered around the room, studying the screen's carvings of birds and flowers.

She'd nearly examined all the screens, and was just moving to the last when she turned her head and discovered Zayed in the doorway watching her.

She hadn't realized he'd arrived and the surprise quickened her pulse, making her suddenly shy. "I didn't hear you."

He entered the room with that stealthy grace of his and in the candlelit room his hair gleamed onyx and his skin a burnished gold. "Have you been waiting long?"

"No. Just a few minutes. I was admiring the screens."

He glanced at one of the ornate screens. "I like them, too. They're one of my favorite antiques here in the palace. They're Moroccan, and date from the sixteenth century. They were used in the harem as room dividers."

"No wonder they're so gorgeous," she said lightly to cover her nervousness. "Beautiful ladies had to be surrounded by beautiful things."

Zayed took a seat on the plump cushions before the table and gestured for her to join him on a pillow close to his. "Show me what you have."

She sat carefully but awkwardly on the turquoise silk pillow he'd gestured to and blushed as her skirt rode up on her thighs. The hem wasn't short but she also wasn't used to showing a lot of leg, and she tried to hide her legs by opening the portfolio.

"These are the first ten profiles the program has matched you with," she said, striving to sound brisk and professional. "Altogether I have thirty possibilities for you, but I only brought twenty profiles and you have them batched in groups of ten."

She handed him the stack of photos with brief bios attached and watched as he silently leafed through them, reading the name, looking at each picture and then skimming the bio. He said nothing until he'd come to the end.

"Nothing?" she asked, prepared to give him the next ten.

"No. I can see there are definitely possibilities."

"Good." She tried to sound hearty and happy, but she wasn't happy. She didn't like doing this. And it was completely unreasonable, but she didn't want him to like any of the women.

She wanted him to like her.

Which was horrible. Ridiculous. Impossible.

Impossible, she fiercely reminded herself as he handed the stack of ten back to her.

"Give me your expert opinion," he said. "Pick out your three favorites from this group. Which are the top three you'd pick for me?"

Her hand shook ever so slightly as she smoothed the pages into a neat stack. "You want *me* to pick?"

"Three women you think would be perfect for me."

She looked up at him, her heart thumping, her stomach churning like mad. "I can't do that."

His dark gold eyes bored into hers. "Why not?"

"I'm not you."

"So?"

"I don't have the same values or tastes. What I like isn't what you'd like."

"You don't know that."

She flashed back to the wretched e-mail Zayed had written to Sharif, the one where he'd mocked her and said he found her so dull. "Oh, but I do," she answered, remembering how she'd loved the night of Lady Pippa's wedding and how she'd enjoyed Zayed's company immensely, and yet he'd been bored to tears.

Zayed sighed his frustration. "I'm not looking for a love connection, just compatibility."

"Fine." Cheeks burning, she flipped through the profiles and selected Jeanette Gardnier, a beautiful brunette French-Canadian law professor; Sarah O'Leary, a stunning redhead journalist from Dublin; and Giselle Sanchez, a golden-brunette corporate banker from Buenos Aires. "There. Three brilliant, strong, successful, independent women. And they're also all tens. Exceptionally beautiful every one."

But he didn't take the profiles. He just looked at her. "Why these women?"

Rou hated how her eyes burned and her throat ached. She hated how this trip had become endless emotion. "They're what you asked for."

His brows pulled. "You're upset."

"I'm not upset."

"Then why won't you look at me?"

"I don't need to look at you."

"You're near tears," he said with some surprise.

"Please." She averted her head, bit her lip, feeling utterly betrayed by her own emotions and weaknesses. She was supposed to be a woman of science. She was supposed to be focused and dedicated to her craft.

Zayed reached out and brushed his fingertip beneath her eye, catching a small single tear. "You're crying."

"I'm not." And yet her chest felt tight and pressure was building behind her eyes. She shouldn't have come here, shouldn't have ever agreed to this horrible, awful proposition. She was impervious to men, all men but Zayed Fehr apparently.

He turned the tip of his finger toward her so she could see the tear. "What is this then?"

"It's a tear."

"Why?"

"*Why?*" Her voice sharpened indignantly. "Because I'm sad, that's why. I am a woman and I do have feelings. And maybe you think I'm a museum or a robot, but I'm not. I never have been." She shook her head, undone. How could she function like this? How could she think like this? She could only be a cool, controlled, logical scientist if she were in a cool, controlled, logical environment, which this wasn't. Ever since Zayed had appeared at her hotel in Vancouver she felt pushed and pressed, torn and stressed. It was madness, and it was reckless, and she had never felt so stupid.

"I've never said anything to imply that you're a robot."

"No, you just think I'm like a museum of science, dull, dull, dull!"

Her words were greeted by silence. Zayed's eyes narrowed and after a moment he spoke. "You knew?"

She flushed, already regretting her outburst. "Sharif didn't mean for me to find out. I wish I hadn't found out."

"That's why you hate me so much."

"You probably thought you were being funny, but it hurt—"

He cut off the rest by reaching for her and covering her mouth with his. Rou stiffened, shocked, and her hands moved to his chest to push him away. And yet his chest felt warm and the broad planes were hard beneath her hands. She could feel the thud of his heartbeat and smell the spice of his skin. The press of her palms turned to something else and she found herself clasping his robe instead.

Zayed's lips had been gentle until that moment, but as if sensing surrender, his kiss hardened, deepened, moving over hers with a fierceness that left her breathless.

Rou had been kissed, but never like this, never with so much heat or hunger or blatant aggression and her head spun and her senses swam.

The pressure of his mouth parted hers and his tongue flicked slowly at her tingling lower lip before curling inside her warm, soft mouth, tasting, possessing, sending shock waves of hot, sharp, dizzying sensation throughout her body.

This had to stop, she thought woozily, she had to stop it, but her body refused to act. It was feeling too many strange and wonderful things, from her heavy useless limbs to the weakness of her muscles. Even her heart seemed to have slowed, thudding with a maddening tempo, a tempo echoed by the shivers licking her spine and the curling, coiling sensation in her belly.

The curling, coiling sensation in her belly was the most maddening. It made her ache deeply, inwardly, made her realize how empty she'd been, how empty she felt.

It was the arrival of the palace butler that ended the kiss. Rou hadn't even heard the man arrive, but Zayed did, and he ended the kiss and untangled himself from Rou with impressive speed.

While the butler spoke quietly to Zayed, Rou swayed on the pillow, definitely not in control. She heard Zayed ask a question but she had no idea what he or the butler were saying. It wasn't until the butler retreated that Zayed turned back to her. "I have to go," he said bluntly.

Rou forced herself to focus on Zayed's chin and then his mouth and then finally his eyes. "Okay."

Zayed reached out, touched her cheek, before frowning and drawing his hand away. "My mother's collapsed. She's been taken to the hospital."

Rou blinked, and little by little everything was slipping back into place, everything except her blood, which still raced hot and sweet in her veins. "Will she be all right?"

"I'm sure she will be. It's just shock. She took the news badly about Sharif's plane."

"Of course she would." Rou expected Zayed to leave, but he hadn't moved yet.

Instead he sat where he was, his expression brooding as he studied her flushed face. He seemed to be choosing his next words with care. "That e-mail…those things I wrote…they were not meant for you."

She knew that. But that didn't make them any less hurtful. "I know."

"I didn't mean to hurt you."

She felt an ache inside her chest. She didn't want his apology, not now. She just wished things were different. That she was different. That she was more beautiful, more vivacious, more appealing. "The e-mail wasn't meant for me. I know."

"But it must have hurt."

Her lips parted but she couldn't make a sound. The e-mail had hurt, terribly. She'd liked him, had imagined he'd liked her, had imagined ridiculous romantic things, but that was three years ago. A long time ago. It didn't matter anymore. "It's in the past. I've moved on."

"I think we should talk about it, but now isn't the time—"

"I don't want to talk about it, and you need to go. Your mother needs you, and I have much to do." Rou struggled to her feet, aware that she couldn't do anything gracefully if she tried. "I'll go back to my room and contact the three women I've selected, and will work on arranging for them to meet you."

He, too, rose but his movements were fluid, elegant, powerful. "I'll come see you when I return from the hospital."

"Not necessary. You've much to do, and I have my work. I'm not here on vacation, I do have a job to do."

He didn't look happy. "I'll have dinner sent to your suite."

"I'm the last one you need to worry about. Just go."

He gave her a long look and then walked out, white robes flowing, broad shoulders very straight. Rou watched him a moment and then, trying not to think of the kiss, or the strange tenderness of her lips, or of the way her blood still felt thick and hot in her veins, gathered her notebooks and profiles and headed back to her room.

CHAPTER FIVE

As THE limousine pulled away from the hospital, Zayed tipped his head against the leather seat and closed his eyes. Now that he knew his mother was fine, that she'd only collapsed to force him to her side, he could turn his attention to other matters. Like the coronation ceremony. And the wife he still needed—a wife his mother said she could conjure tomorrow if need be. And Rou.

Rou.

Why did he kiss her? What on earth possessed him to kiss Rou Tornell? *Dr.* Tornell?

She wasn't a woman he'd ever found particularly attractive. He hadn't ever wanted to kiss her, and yet the kiss…

The kiss surprised him. It was hot.

Explosive.

Nothing like he'd imagined. But then she wasn't quite what he'd imagined, either.

And she'd known about his e-mail to Sharif following Pippa's wedding. She knew he'd rejected her, and while he didn't recall the exact words he'd used, he knew the tone of his e-mail had probably been sarcastic, if not mocking.

Zayed winced in the darkness. He shouldn't have behaved so unkindly. He certainly hadn't meant to hurt her. If anything, he'd been making a dig at Sharif. Sharif and his geeky little protégée. Sharif and all his lost causes.

Zayed briefly closed his eyes, ashamed of himself. But this was nothing new. He lived with shame. He'd brought the curse on himself. It was his actions that had cursed them all.

The guilt was often unbearable and for the past fifteen years he'd tried to destroy himself, make dust out of dust but nothing he did, nothing he took, nothing he tried worked. He failed at failing. God wouldn't let him die.

But God didn't let him live, either.

Instead, his world was one of jaded material pleasures—fast cars, fast times, fast women. He indulged every whim, partook of every vice, and enjoyed none of it.

But now he was back in Isi, Sarq's capital city, back in the place he'd grown up. He was here to take the place of his brother. Here to make amends. If he could make amends.

If only he could break the curse. Save what was left of his family.

If only.

Ten minutes later, the limousine turned down the long drive leading to the palace gates. Zayed shifted restlessly.

He'd have to go see Rou. He'd told her he'd stop by when he returned. If only he hadn't kissed her.

If only he'd kept his distance he wouldn't have discovered that her icy scientist image was just a facade.

Slim, blond Rou Tornell wasn't a cold-blooded scientist. She was a woman. A woman he'd very much enjoyed kissing.

Back at the palace, Zayed headed straight to Rou's suite. The lights were still on and, descending the steps into her sunken living room, he saw the living room was empty but a series of heavy silver trays covered the low table. He lifted the lids on the dishes, discovering little pots of aromatic rice; plates of grilled, skewered meats; a copper bowl of sizzling, sautéed prawns; platters of steamed, seasoned fish; cooked vegetable dishes of potatoes, peas and artichoke hearts. All untouched. Had she eaten nothing?

He was just about to walk out when he heard a rustle of paper. Turning, he spotted her at her desk. She'd fallen asleep while working, her right hand still on the keyboard, her left arm and cheek resting on her stack of notebooks.

Zayed took a step toward her and then another. She still wore that hideous gray suit, but her hair was unpinned and it spilled over her arm in a sheet of silver and pale gold. Asleep, her face was soft, her lips full and curved. Asleep, she looked alarmingly vulnerable.

He never took advantage of vulnerable women. He never took advantage of any woman.

Why had he kissed her?

Perplexed, he nearly left her as she was, but then guilt battered his conscience. She was here because he'd asked for her help. The least he could do was send her to bed.

He placed a light hand on her shoulder. "Dr. Tornell, wake up. You need to go to bed."

She barely stirred and didn't waken. He touched her shoulder again, shook her gently. "Rou."

This time his voice registered and she sleepily lifted her head to look at him. "Hi."

Hi. So American, so informal, so unlike who he thought Rou Tornell was.

His gaze skimmed her bare face, with the soft, full mouth and the long eyelashes that were surprisingly dark and thick. Without thinking he brushed the side of his hand across her cheek. Her skin was as warm and soft as it looked. "It's after midnight. Time for you to go to bed."

She sat up abruptly, remembering. "How's your mom?"

"Brittle. Hysterical. Exhausting." He shrugged. "But then she's always been that way."

She yawned and pushed a wave of pale hair from her face, her cheeks still flushed pink from sleep. "That doesn't sound very nice."

"She's not what I'd call nice."

Rou now frowned. "You don't have a good relationship with her?"

He sat down on a corner of the desk. "Tonight was the first time I'd seen her in years."

"Why?"

"She's controlling. Manipulative. I saw how she treated Sharif and his family. Vowed I'd never allow that in my life."

"But you went to her tonight?"

He made a soft, rough sound. "She's my mother."

Rou's lips twisted. "If I didn't know you better, I'd say you were a good man."

He smiled crookedly. "Fortunately, you do."

"Fortunately."

Zayed felt a tug in his chest. The tug was strong and it almost hurt. "I am sorry about earlier—"

"Forgotten."

One eyebrow lifted. "The kiss, or the e-mail?"

"Both."

"That easily?"

Her shoulders lifted and fell. "I compartmentalize."

"Ah, you're retreating behind the scientist mask."

"It's not a mask. It's who I am. It's what I do."

"And the kiss? Means nothing?"

"Absolutely nothing," she answered firmly. "You're stressed. I'm stressed. We made a mistake. It's over, done, behind us."

"But it was good."

She colored vividly, blood rushing to her cheeks. "I wouldn't know," she answered primly.

He laughed softly, despite the endless, exhausting day. She was so provoking and yet strangely entertaining. And before he could think better of it, he reached out to trace the plane of her face, the cheek-bone and jawline, her small straight nose and the curve of her upper lip.

She pulled away. "I'm not one of your three candidates, Sheikh Fehr!"

If she'd hoped to freeze him with her frigid tone and cool lecture she'd failed. "Perhaps you should be," he answered mildly.

Rou pushed up from the desk. "We're in the middle of a crisis here—"

"And I should be taking it more seriously?" he finished for her, thinking he liked this Rou Tornell far more than the scientist mask she presented to the world.

Angry, she was fierce and alive, feminine and strong. Prickly, too, but it suited her. Made her volatile. Feisty. Passionate.

"Yes," she agreed adamantly, her long, pale hair tumbling down her back, her breasts rising and falling beneath the tailored coat.

Make that feisty, passionate and hot, he mentally corrected, letting his gaze slide over her slim figure, down her hips to her bare legs, lingering on those legs. They were even more shapely without heels, and he found himself fantasizing about what he could do with legs like that.

A kiss to the knee. A kiss behind the knee. A kiss to the pulse behind that lovely knee when she trembled.

And she'd tremble. Women always did, but she, Rou Tornell, would most definitely tremble. He knew that now, knew that Rou Tornell was nothing like the image she projected.

"Having spent the past three hours listening to my mother wail, I'm very aware of the current crisis. However, I'm also a man, and you're a woman—"

"No."

"No?"

She blushed wildly. "I mean, yes, I am a woman, but not the right woman for you. I'm not your type. I'll never be your type. It has to do with laws of attraction."

He could still feel the warmth and softness of her mouth beneath his fingertip. "Laws of attraction?"

"It's my field of study." She pushed a long, silvery tendril of hair behind her ear. "The science and chemistry of romantic love. It's an unconscious drive, something the brain controls through chemicals and hormones."

"And you don't think my brain could find you attractive?"

"No."

The edge of his mouth lifted, quirking. "You know an awful lot about my brain."

"I know men are prone to impulse, particularly the sexual impulse, but that doesn't mean true attraction, or compatibility. And that, Sheikh Fehr, is what we're interested in. Compatibility, synergy, marriage."

He nodded when she finished, but he wasn't actually listening anymore. She'd lost him about the time she mentioned sexual impulse because sex was on his mind, and to his way of thinking, she was a woman in desperate need of proper lovemaking. He couldn't imagine the last time she'd been bedded, and yet that's exactly what she needed. After a couple hours between the sheets, after a couple orgasms, she'd look entirely different. She'd carry herself differently. Her blue gaze would be softer. Her color would be high. And that mouth, that sweet, full mouth, would be swollen from kisses.

If he weren't in such a bind, if he didn't need a wife, he'd enjoy teaching Dr. Rou Tornell about the side of love she didn't lecture on...and that was the physical. Love was more than textbook science. It was also skill, patience and desire.

"I'm here to find you a wife," she added shortly. "That is it."

"Right." He cocked his head, considered her legs, her silken tumble of hair, the dark pink staining her cheeks and smiled wickedly.

"So we're in perfect understanding? We will keep our relationship professional. We won't indulge in any more touches, kisses, flirtations. This is business, and there's a science to the business—"

"I was wrong about you, you know. You're very interesting. And very appealing, especially when you're in a righteous mood." He smiled. "A man likes a proper challenge. And you, my buttoned-down, uptight, prudish Dr. Tornell, are a proper challenge." With a last smile in her direction, he left.

Rou tumbled into the living room and down onto

the white couch the moment Zayed disappeared and reached for a ruby pillow to squeeze against her chest. *Buttoned-down. Uptight. Prudish?*

How dare he? How crass. How arrogant. How perfectly Zayed Fehr!

There was no way she could find a good wife for him. No decent woman would take him. He was horrible. Arrogant. Sexual.

Sexual. And then she bit her lip and closed her eyes and tried to block out the way he'd kissed her and the way her body had responded and the way she imagined making love would be.

It'd be good.

Maybe even great.

Oh, God. She had to get out of here.

In bed, it took forever for Rou to relax. She tossed and turned so long that she eventually turned the light on and reached for a book, but even the book couldn't hold her attention.

The problem was Zayed. The problem was his kiss. The problem was she still felt too warm and so emotionally and physically stirred.

That kiss was unlike any kiss she'd ever experienced. It had made her ache and burn. Made her want to take things further. She'd never enjoyed sex before, but with Zayed she knew it'd be different. Everything with him was different.

With him she didn't feel frigid. She felt. She wanted. She *needed*. Desired. Hungered.

She'd always been accused of being so cerebral, and maybe it was her own fear that kept her emotions and desires in check, but her body hadn't ever been important. Yet tonight when Zayed kissed her, her body stunned her by coming to life, expressing needs. Wants. Demands.

She found the revelation both wonderful and awful. Wonderful because she relished feeling alive. Wonderful because she'd never felt this way before. And yet awful because she knew once she left here, she'd never feel this again.

It was close to three before she fell asleep, and nearing eight when she woke. Her head ached and she groggily stumbled from bed to the living room to look out the French doors where the sun was still rising and painting the sky shades of pink and rose.

Still wearing her cozy, pale blue pajamas, Rou pulled her hair into a messy ponytail, plopped on her glasses and grabbed her laptop. She carried it to the couch and opened her e-mail to see if she'd gotten any responses yet.

None of the three women she'd contacted last night had responded to her e-mail yet, and instead of being disappointed she felt relief. Not that she was supposed to feel relief. She was here to do a job and she was failing. That wasn't good.

To combat her guilt, Rou wondered if she should send another batch of e-mail invites, but then admitted that her efforts were futile at best.

There was no way she was going to come up with a

bride for him in twenty-four or thirty-six hours. No way a sane woman would hop on the royal jet, arrive here, talk to Zayed for sixty minutes and agree to marriage.

Instead there had to be someone else, someone closer, someone already familiar with Zayed Fehr. An ex-girlfriend perhaps. A friend of the family's. A second or third cousin.

She was just opening one of her spiral notebooks to begin brainstorming when a soft knock sounded outside her suite.

"Come in," Rou called, hoping it was Manar with coffee and some biscuits.

Instead a pretty brunette in a simple belted cream dress appeared between the columns. She stood at the top of the stairs and smiled wanly at Rou. "I haven't been a very good hostess. I'm so sorry. I should have welcomed you earlier. I'm Jesslyn Fehr—"

"Queen Fehr!" Rou was on her feet and rushing forward to greet Sharif's wife, who was descending the stairs into the sunken living room. Rou didn't know if she was expected to bow or curtsy. "I don't expect you to play hostess while I'm here. Never. I already feel bad intruding during this time. I know you have so much to deal with right now."

Jesslyn's hand lifted, fell. She looked dazed, lost. "Unfortunately, I don't actually have enough to do. I'm finding it hard to stay busy. Nothing lets me forget. Not even the children."

Up close, Rou saw the strain in the queen's face,

her pallor, and the deep shadows beneath her eyes and lines at the creases. "How are you?"

Jesslyn tried to smile and failed. "He has to come back. I can't do this without him."

"Come, sit." Rou gestured to the couch. "And I'm sorry I'm not dressed. I was enjoying working in my pajamas."

"The best way to work," the queen answered. "When I was a teacher I spent entire weekends in my pajamas grading papers." Jesslyn took a seat on the couch opposite Rou's. "Have you had coffee? Anything to eat?"

"I'm fine—"

"I haven't had breakfast, either, and would enjoy sitting here, talking to you, while we had a bite." She paused. "If you don't mind."

Rou could see why Sharif loved Jesslyn, and her heart squeezed with grief. Jesslyn was beautiful but real, humble and down-to-earth. "I wouldn't mind. Not at all."

Jesslyn leaned over and pressed a nearly invisible button on the leg of the low coffee table. Almost immediately a robed attendant appeared. "Yes, Your Highness?"

"Mehta, could we perhaps have coffee for two? And if Cook has any of his breakfast pastries, a few of those would be nice, too."

Jesslyn glanced around the living room after her attendant left. "I haven't been here in a while. This is where I stayed when I first came to the palace. But it's still beautiful with the courtyard and the morning sun."

Rou followed the queen's gaze. "It's an extraordinary suite."

"Have you been outside yet? Explored the garden?"

"No, but I should. I'll make sure to go out later this morning."

The queen nodded absently. "It was their room, you know."

"Whose?"

Jesslyn turned to look at her, her eyes filled with sadness. "The girls. The twins. Jamila and Aman. These rooms are rarely used. I think you and I have been the only ones to stay here since they died."

Rou was shocked. She'd had no idea. "You were friends with them?"

"Best friends. We met in school and then later shared a flat. We were all on holiday in Greece when the accident happened." Her lips tightened. "They died a week apart. It's how I met Sharif. At the hospital, the day before Aman died."

She blinked, looked across at Rou. "I can't lose him. I can't live without him. He's everything. He's my hope and my heart." Tears filled her eyes but she blinked them back, and forced a smile as well as a turn in the conversation. "I understand you know Sharif."

Rou had to blink back tears of her own. "Yes. I earned the Fehr scholarship when I was at Cambridge. Over time I got to know your husband, the king. He was a wonderful mentor, very kind, very generous."

Jesslyn's expression cleared. "You're the psychologist?"

Rou nodded, a lump in her throat. "Yes."

"And now you and Zayed have found each other. How wonderful. Isn't it funny how the world works? Sharif once told me that good can always come of bad, and maybe he's right. Maybe good will somehow come out of all of this."

Mehta arrived with a tray of coffee, and Manar was right behind her with a pitcher of freshly squeezed orange juice, a plate of fragrant, flaky pastries, and bowls of thick creamy yogurt.

They were still together, sipping coffee and talking about the children and how two-year-old Tahir, Sharif and Jesslyn's son, was into everything, when Zayed arrived a half hour later.

Zayed immediately went to Jesslyn and kissed her on each cheek and then he turned and greeted Rou. "What? No gray suit today?"

Dressed in dark slacks and a white linen shirt, his dark hair damp and jaw freshly shaved, he exuded cool and sophistication, which only made Rou feel even more frumpish.

"I just haven't had a chance to put it on yet," she answered, painfully self-conscious. It was bad enough to receive the queen of Sarq in her pajamas and glasses, but now Zayed, too?

"As much as I like the gray suit, you might want a change of clothes. It's going to be very hot today and

I'd thought perhaps I'd show you around the palace gardens later."

"You two have much to do, so I'll leave you now," Jesslyn said, setting aside her cup and rising. She kissed Zayed and then smiled warmly at Rou. "I'll be taking the children swimming later. If you get a moment free, you're more than welcome to join us. The children are dying to meet their new aunt." And then with another smile she left, leaving Zayed and Rou staring at each other.

"What did she just say?" Rou choked, as soon as Jesslyn was well out of earshot. *"Aunt?"*

Zayed's forehead creased deeply, and he glanced toward the corridor where Jesslyn had disappeared. "I heard that, too."

"It was a mistake. I'm sure she didn't even know what she was saying." Rou reached up to tug the elastic from her hair, letting the pale strands fall loose over her shoulders. "Right?"

Zayed's hands went to his hips and he continued to stare off in the direction Jesslyn had gone. "I don't know."

"What do you mean, you don't know? How could she think we...I..." She took a quick breath. "She knows I'm a psychologist, a relationship expert, she knows I'm here working with you."

Silence stretched until Rou's nerves felt close to breaking, and then he turned and looked at her and shrugged. "Maybe she doesn't. Maybe she believes you're my fiancée."

"How can that be?"

He shrugged calmly. "I said the next time I returned, I'd come with my fiancée."

Rou stared at him, horrified. "Does everyone think that?"

"I don't know. It would explain why you're here in my sisters' rooms. These rooms are reserved for immediate family only."

"Oh no." Rou covered her eyes, not wanting to imagine what Jesslyn was thinking as they sat here having breakfast together, talking about life and children, work and the future. Had Jesslyn imagined that Rou was her future sister-in-law? Oh, so awkward, especially as Jesslyn already had so much to cope with.

She dropped her hands. "You have to go explain," she said urgently. "You have to go now and make sure everyone knows I'm not your fiancée, but here working to help you get one. Especially the queen. She's so stressed already. I don't want her to feel uncomfortable when your future fiancée does arrive."

"And when is that, Dr. Tornell? This morning? Tonight? Tomorrow? We're no closer to finding a wife for me now than we were in Vancouver five days ago." He dropped onto the couch where Jesslyn had been sitting, folded his arms behind his head and gazed steadily at Rou. "Perhaps it's time to rethink our search."

"I was thinking the same thing." Rou reached for her notepad, ready to take notes. "There must be someone close to you, already in your life, who would be suitable. A former girlfriend. A second or third cousin. A family friend."

He nodded thoughtfully. "A family friend. Yes. Someone that knows us, someone with a history with us. That would make the most sense." Zayed leaned forward, snagged a pastry from the nearly full tray and took a bite. "Be ideal, actually."

"Good. I'm glad we're in agreement," she said, making a few more notes on her pad of paper. "But tell me, I'm curious. Sharif has four children, three girls and a boy, two-year-old Tahir. Why wouldn't one of them inherit the throne? Why does it pass to you?"

"It's due to our old Sarq laws. In many ways we're a modern country, but in other ways, we have changed very little in the past four hundred years, and Sarq tradition dictates that it must be a male ruler, and he must have reached the mature age of twenty-five, as well as be married with at least one wife—"

"At least one wife?" Her head jerked up. "How many wives are kings expected to have?"

"My father and grandfather were forward-thinking men and they both only took one wife. My great-grandfather had three."

"But a king today could have more than one wife?"

"Legally, yes. Morally? No. For the past one hundred years, Fehrs have taken just one wife, and loved one wife. We are loyal to our women, and I— despite what you may have heard about me—will be loyal, too."

"I suppose that would be a relief for your future wife."

He smiled. "I thought so, too."

"Now, do you have someone in mind, or are we to brainstorm and start a list?"

His expression turned lazy. "Oh, I have someone in mind."

"Excellent." Now they were getting somewhere, and she smiled at him expectantly.

He smiled back even more pleasantly. "I think you'll be surprised."

"Really?"

"Yes. I've decided on you."

Her pulse did a funny little flutter. Clearly she wasn't following his logic. "Excuse me?"

"I've decided on you, Dr. Tornell. You're perfect. Educated, accomplished, successful. And best of all, you're an old family friend. Brother Sharif's protégée."

Rou stumbled to her feet, putting distance between them. "Have you been drinking?"

"I had a coffee, but it wasn't an espresso."

"Sheikh Fehr—"

"Perhaps it's time you called me Zayed."

Her voice hardened. "Sheikh Fehr—"

"We are virtually betrothed."

Rou's head swam. She sat down abruptly on the stone steps. "No. No, we're not. Absolutely not. Under no condition, in any situation."

"But I'm afraid Jesslyn and the children already believe it to be the case."

She pointed down the hall. "Then go clear up the

misunderstanding. I am here to help you find a wife, and that's the only reason I am here."

"I'll still fund your research center. The money would still be yours."

She, who never swooned, nearly fainted now. Was he serious? And had he really just mentioned money? That he'd give her *money* to marry him?

Rou grabbed the edge of the step with both hands and held on for dear life. Her stomach was doing crazy somersaults. In fact the room was spinning wildly. "We. Are. Not. Marrying."

He just regarded her with lazy calm. "You know you're the perfect solution. You're exactly what I want. You know my situation. You know I need an arranged marriage and am not planning on a love match. You're highly qualified as candidates go, you're smart and interesting and our children would be very bright—"

"Good God! Children?"

"We could wait a year before trying to get you pregnant to see if Sharif is found, because if he returned, I'd of course free you from your obligations...."

"You're serious." Her voice fell to a whisper, and she once again was staggering to her feet, rushing for the privacy and sanctity of her bedroom and bath.

"There's no reason to panic," he called after her. "We'll have the courtship. We'll just begin after the ceremony."

Rou turned in the doorway to her bedroom to look at him. He was still sitting where she'd left him, cool and calm and as confident as could be.

The worst thing was, she couldn't even pretend he was insane. She knew the signs of insanity. He didn't display those. But he was totally, completely out of touch.

She wasn't the marrying kind. She'd never be the marrying kind. Thanks to her parents, she was committed to a life of celibacy. "If you won't talk to Queen Fehr, I will," she said fiercely. "Far better to clear the misunderstanding now than ruin all our lives." She entered the bedroom and quietly but firmly shut the door.

CHAPTER SIX

ROU paced for a few minutes after Zayed left, trying to figure out the best way to handle the situation because Zayed's solution to the problem—*marriage*—wasn't a solution no matter how you looked at it.

Although, she supposed that wasn't entirely true. From Zayed's perspective, if she married him, his problem was solved. He had a wife, he had a throne. He had it made.

She, on the other hand, gained nothing by marrying Sheikh Fehr. She loved her life. It was a great life, especially as she had no intention of ever getting married, and marriage was fine for other people, people who wanted a domestic life dominated by children and family. But that wasn't for her. She loved work, needed her work, and there was no way she'd give up her career—her calling—for a man, much less a man like Zayed Fehr.

What she had to do was talk to Queen Jesslyn. Once Jesslyn knew the truth, Zayed couldn't coerce her into marriage.

Although Rou dreaded going to Jesslyn now, especially after their breakfast together. Jesslyn had been so raw, so grief-stricken that it seemed unfair to hit her with one more thing now.

Rou closed her eyes briefly, sick at adding to Jesslyn's burden, but what else could she do? Let Zayed manipulate her into marriage?

Never.

Although…and she'd never admit this to anyone, a tiny part of her *was* curious. *Curious* wasn't the right word. *Flattered* might be better. It wasn't as if she had hordes of gorgeous, sexy men in their prime beating down her door.

As a matter of fact there were no men beating on her door, and she was attracted to Zayed, terribly attracted. She'd spent most of the night tossing and turning as she fantasized about making love with him. Now a marriage proposal.

Not that she'd ever consider it.

No, she'd just have to talk to Jesslyn, and the sooner the better.

Rou allowed Manar to fill the gigantic marble tub in the equally gigantic bathroom for her. Rou would have preferred a quick, brisk shower but it wasn't an option, and once Manar left her to bathe in privacy, Rou slipped out of her pajamas and into the steaming tub fragrant with vanilla and spice.

Rou almost laughed as she settled deep into the water. This was all so Arabian Nights, and if she were a different woman, she might be tempted to savor such luxury. Might even be tempted by Zayed's proposal.

But she *was* a different woman, and she'd been raised with money, and she'd grown up in a sprawling mansion in Beverly Hills with maids and cooks, personal assistants and chauffeurs. And money didn't buy happiness. Money didn't protect love. Money just made people arrogant and selfish, petty and nasty.

While she worked with people who were wealthy, she never craved their toys, their bank accounts or their lifestyles. As long as she could provide for herself, material things were not her goal. What she wanted, needed, was independence. Confidence. Self-respect. She craved a world of her own, one in which she could control the emotions around her, including her own. Something she couldn't do if she remained here in Sarq.

Out of the bath, Rou rubbed herself briskly with the towel and considered her limited wardrobe options. She'd brought her suitcase from Vienna, a suitcase that had also carried her tour clothes in Portland, Seattle and Vancouver, clothes intended for cool days and cooler nights. Cashmeres and woolens. Turtle-necks and dark, heavy fabrics. Nothing appropriate for desert temperatures.

She ended up in her black suit only because she could pair the severe skirt with a black knit top that was short-sleeved. Dressed in low heels, long hair in its traditional knot at the back of her head, she set off to find the queen.

Jesslyn and the children hadn't made it to the pool yet. Instead they were all in the children's nursery, where Sharif's girls from his first marriage were playing Monopoly, and two-year-old terror Prince Tahir was trying to knock all the pieces off the board. The girls would admonish him but it just made him giggle. For her part, Queen Jesslyn sat nearby, watching, and yet clearly not present.

Mehta, Jesslyn's maid, had walked Rou to the nursery door, but now that Rou was there, she wished she hadn't insisted on coming. This family was fighting like mad for normalcy. Their world had been turned upside down these past few weeks, and suddenly Rou despised herself for being at the nursery door, an outsider. An intruder.

"Mama," Tahir said, spotting Rou first. "Mama, lady, look."

Jesslyn jerked, turned to see where her toddler was pointing and discovered Rou in the doorway. "Oh, Rou. Hello. Come in. I'm sorry, I didn't see you there." She smiled at Rou as Tahir clambered onto her lap.

Rou saw the queen's hand tremble as she reached up to stroke her son's dark curls.

Rou's heart seized. She shouldn't be here, shouldn't have come.

"Girls," Jesslyn said, injecting a note of cheer into her voice, "I'd like you to meet someone very special. This is Uncle Zayed's fiancée, Dr. Rou Tornell. They're to be married tomorrow. Isn't that exciting?"

The girls, ranging in age from nine to eleven, stood and bowed respectfully, and yet their dark eyes were full of curiosity.

Jesslyn introduced the children, and afterward, Jinan, the eldest, asked if Rou was going to be married Western style, or in a traditional Sarq ceremony.

Rou's brain froze. This is what she'd come to straighten out, and yet she couldn't move, couldn't speak, all words trapped in her throat as she felt the weight of five pairs of eyes rest on her.

Say something, she told herself. *Explain the situation. Just say, there's been a misunderstanding. Just say, I'm not marrying your uncle, I'd never marry your uncle.*

But she couldn't. She couldn't find her voice, not when the room ached with sadness.

It was Takia, the nine-year-old, who finally broke the silence. "You're not waiting for Daddy to come home? You're getting married without him?"

For a moment the room was so quiet you could hear a pin drop, and then the stillness gave way to grief. The queen cried silently, but Saba and Jinan sobbed, and Tahir, confused, threw his arms around his mother and howled.

Only Takia stayed silent as she stared at Rou, her eyes enormous, her small mouth compressed.

Rou, who hated feelings, hated emotion, hated grief, felt as though her heart was being ripped into pieces. Children shouldn't know pain. Children shouldn't have to grow up quickly. And yet these children had been thrust into reality at a very young age, their loss all the more tragic in that the girls had already lost their mother several years before.

"I wish we could wait for your father," Rou said huskily. "It won't be a very nice wedding without him."

"Maybe we should wait," Takia whispered.

"Uncle Zayed and Aunt Rou want that, too," Jesslyn answered, looking over Tahir's head at the girls, "but the country is in turmoil without Daddy, and no one can make any decisions without a king, and Uncle Zayed is being very good and brave, and he's doing what Daddy would want."

"And that's to marry Aunt Rou?" Saba guessed.

Jesslyn smiled through her tears. "And become king."

Rou couldn't stay. She threw a desperate, panicked smile at them and ran out, aware that she was going to lose her composure any second. She'd barely made it out the door before the tears began to fall. It was all too much, too intense, too horrible.

Their grief made Sharif's death real and it hit Rou hard, so very hard. Sharif was gone. Dead. He wasn't coming back.

Sharif, the man she'd adored for a decade or more, was gone.

And now, wiping away tears, she struggled to find her way back to her wing of the palace. She made a couple of turns, and then another and before she knew it, she realized she was lost. She didn't even know how to get back to her wing.

She was close to flagging down a palace servant when she stumbled into Zayed.

"I've just been to your room," he said, catching her by the arm and steadying her.

"I went to see the queen," she answered, wiping tears.

"What's wrong? Has something happened?"

"Your brother's dead. The queen and her children are heartbroken. The country's in turmoil, and you're being brave and good and helping out by becoming king." She glared up at him even as the tears continued to fall. "What am I to do? Tell them I'm not marrying you? Tell them there won't be a wedding, and their country won't have a king? Queen Jesslyn introduced me to the children as Aunt Rou, for heaven's sake! I'm their aunt now. And the little one, Takia, didn't understand why we weren't waiting for her daddy before we married!"

Her stream of tortured words ended and she looked at him for help.

"How could I have ever thought you unemotional?" he said.

"Well, I don't like being this way—"

"I like you this way. You're real. And you're exactly what's needed."

She bit her lip to keep it from quivering like Takia's.

"But if I could, I'd undo all this," he added quietly. "I would give anything to see Sharif walk through those doors. I would give up everything I own, everything I am, to have him home safe. But until that day, I must do what he needs me to do. And that includes marrying and assuming the throne. But I need you to fulfill my duty. I can't do it without you."

"Not me, a wife."

"But you are that wife. You're the one I want. You're the one I need."

She pictured Jesslyn and the children in the nursery and tears welled up all over again. Love, loss, marriage, children...the palace was full of everything that she feared most.

Family.

Pain.

And yet she couldn't walk away from a family in such pain. She'd spent years going to school, years building her private practice, years counseling and listening, years writing, speaking, years dedicated to helping others. How could she just run away when there was so much need right here?

She averted her head. "I need some time," she whispered, shaken.

He started to argue and then, after a deep breath, nodded. "We'll meet for a late lunch. That should give you a couple hours."

"That's not enough."

"It has to be. I—we—Sarq, we're running out of time. This country hasn't had a king in nearly two weeks. Decisions can't be made, not even about my brother's funeral."

"All right." She knew her voice was sharp but she was tired and overwhelmed. Nothing was as it was supposed to be. And if she wasn't careful, nothing would ever be again.

"I'll take you back to your rooms."

"No, just point me in the right direction."

"It's complicated."

"I'm smart."

Their eyes met, gazes locking, both frustrated and furious.

After a long moment of tense silence, Zayed lifted his hands. "Fine. You win. Continue down this corridor to the second hall, take a left, and then at the first right, turn. Continue to the second hall, and then a left and then another left, one more right, and then you'll be back in your wing. Got that?"

She smiled. "Piece a cake." Not at all, but he didn't need to know it.

In the end, Rou had to stop two different palace staff members to get clarification on the directions, but she did eventually arrive at her suite, and once there, she went to the bedroom and stretched out, pulling a soft pillow beneath her cheek.

The bed was so comfortable and pretty, with silk and satin curtains in every shade of rose surrounding the antique frame, that she could almost imagine Zayed's sisters here. It was a room fit for princesses, and that's what his sisters had been. But they were gone, and now Sharif was, too.

It was all too much being here, all too intense, too emotional and just too sad.

No wonder Zayed's mother had collapsed and been rushed to the hospital. How could any mother bear to lose so many of her children?

Although Rou wanted nothing more than to hop on the next plane and jet back to San Francisco, she reluctantly accepted that it wasn't an option. Zayed was right. He did need her. But she wasn't going to give up who she was, or what she wanted, not forever, not even for Zayed, although she now knew she wanted to help.

But marriage?

Perhaps if it was just a temporary marriage…something to get them through the next couple of weeks…

She must have eventually fallen asleep because Manar was there, waking her up, reminding her lunch was in just a half hour, and wouldn't she like to dress before she met His Highness on the terrace?

Rou sat up, groggy, and rubbed her eyes. "It's already one?"

"Yes, Dr. Tornell. You have half an hour till your luncheon."

"Then I have time," Rou said, lying back down and nestling into her pillow. "There's nothing I need to do to get ready."

But Manar didn't move. "Don't you want to pick something else to wear to lunch? The terrace is shaded but it's quite warm still."

"I would if I could," Rou answered with a yawn, "but this is all I have."

"But, Dr. Tornell, come see. You have dozens and dozens of boxes and bags. They've all been flown in from Dubai."

Rou sat back up. "What?"

"They're for your trousseau, but His Highness wants you to start wearing them today. He said you needed something better suited for palace life." The maid gestured, barely able to contain her excitement. "They're all in the living room. Come look."

Rou slid off the bed and padded barefoot into the living room, which was no longer a serene sitting area but a riot of colorful shopping bags. Dozens and dozens of boxes and bags covered the two sofas, with another dozen shoe boxes stacked on the low coffee table. As she descended the steps, she recognized a few of the names—Michael Kors, Chanel, Prada, Valentino, Dior—and then there were names she didn't recognize, but the boxes and tissue were equally formal and impressive.

Uncertainly she lifted the lid on the garment box closest to her and discovered a frothy pink cocktail dress.

Pale pink peeked through the crisp tissue paper in the next box, this time in the softest cardigan imaginable, with diamond buttons.

Holding her breath now, she opened another box and she lifted a pleated coral silk dress with a thin gold chain at the waist.

Another box, a slim white skirt, the palest pink gladiator-style shoe, a pink crocodile clutch.

It was a sea of pink.

Dizzy, Rou sat down on an armchair facing the couches. She didn't wear pink. Ever.

Where was the black, the navy, the charcoal-gray she wore? Where were her serious pieces, the wardrobe that made her feel smart, safe, invincible? These were such girlie, feminine items—skirts and heels, sexy ankle-wrap sandals and figure-hugging fabrics.

"Is everything pink?" she asked Manar, a hint of despair in her voice.

Manar lifted her head. "You don't like your new clothes?"

"They're just so…pink."

Manar gently ran a hand over a hot-pink, silk trench coat lined with a paler shade of satin. "But they're beautiful. Like candy or jewels."

Rou, who rarely cried, felt close to tears for the second time in one day. Candy? Jewels? Did Zayed really buy her clothes that resembled candy and jewels? How could he think she'd like something so silly? So impractical? So unprofessional?

Wardrobe was important. It was image. Status. Power. And with a wardrobe of baby pink, coral, rose and fuchsia, he was turning her into an accessory. She wouldn't allow it. She wouldn't be his doll or arm candy. She was Dr. Rou Tornell, and he'd better not forget it.

To Manar's horror, Rou insisted on wearing her black wool skirt and black knit top to lunch. "Why," the maid exclaimed, "when you have the most beautiful clothes here?"

Rou opened her mouth, but couldn't think of an appropriate explanation. Manar then reached among the piles of pastel-hued accessories and grabbed a jeweler's box containing a long strand of fat, pink pearls. "At least wear these," she begged. "That way you won't appear to be rejecting all of His Highness's gifts."

Rou accepted Manar's offer to take her to the garden where she'd be joining Zayed for lunch. Before she'd even stepped onto the patio she heard the tinkling notes of a fountain. A vine-covered arbor provided shade on the terrace and the sweet scent of antique roses perfumed the air.

Zayed was already there, waiting for her, and despite the terrace's shadows, she could feel the weight of his gaze as she approached. He was studying her the same way she used to study specimens under the microscope, and she stiffened, not enjoying the intense scrutiny.

"You don't like your new clothes?" he asked.

Rou had unpinned her chignon and left her hair loose, but other than that change to her hair, and the addition of her pearls, she looked the same as he'd seen her earlier in the day. "They're all pink, Your Highness," she said, taking the seat he offered her and then carefully spreading the pale lavender linen napkin across her lap.

He took the chair opposite her. "You don't like pink?"

She shot him a level look. "Do I look like a woman that wears pink?"

His gaze held hers and then dropped to her mouth and then lower, down her neck to her breasts, where they seemed to linger indecently long. "You look like a woman that needs to remember she's a woman."

Rou bristled. "And dressing me in pink like a fancy doll will turn me into a proper woman?"

"No. Proper lovemaking should do that, but in the meantime, I see no reason why you shouldn't wear colors and styles that flatter your coloring and complexion. You're a beautiful woman—"

"*Please*, Sheikh Fehr."

"—determined to hide behind the most hideous clothes and styles possible." He stopped, smiled faintly and added, "Do you think we could start using each other's first names now? It seems strange that we're still using titles."

"I like being Dr. Tornell."

He grinned crookedly, gold eyes flashing. "Yes, I know you do. And if it makes you happy, I promise to call you Dr. Tornell in the bedroom."

Rou blushed again, her skin burning from her chest to her brow as she pushed her water glass away from her. "That was so not necessary, *Zayed*," she said, stressing his name.

He just smiled, which only made him even more gorgeous. "You're perfect, Rou. Perfectly proper, perfectly prickly. A rare, delicious fruit covered in dangerous thorns."

Face burning, she forced her attention to the table, where white lush roses spilled from the round centerpiece. "In case you think the thorns are protecting a sweet, delicate pulp, you're mistaken. The inside of me is just as thorny and sour as the exterior."

"I'm sure there's a cure for that."

"I don't want a cure! I like who I am."

"As do I."

She was saved from having to answer by the appearance of kitchen staff as they paraded out with a stream of lunch dishes. Olives in marinade. Roasted red peppers with feta, capers and lemons. Stuffed grape leaves. Stuffed eggplants. Spicy, skewered grilled shrimp. Chilled lentil salad. Warm flat breads. Dish after dish kept arriving, despite the fact that Rou couldn't even manage more than a couple mouthfuls.

Zayed, she noticed, didn't have that problem. He ate generously of everything, enjoying his meal as though he didn't have a care in the world.

He looked up, caught her gaze. "You can't let conflict and tension control you," he said, as if able to read her mind. "You have to learn to separate your emotions from conflict, as conflict will always exist—"

"It didn't before you entered my life," she interrupted tartly. "I was fine. I was happy. I was successful."

"And you are still successful, and you will be happy. You're not losing anything by marrying me. You're gaining a husband, a family and a kingdom."

She shook her head, incredulous. "But I don't want a husband, a family or a kingdom. I like the simplicity of my life. It works for me. It allows me to accomplish the things I do."

"You don't think you can still be successful as a wife? You don't think you can accomplish great things if you become a mother?"

"No. No, I don't," she answered firmly, a quaver in her voice. "And while I might consider a temporary marriage, I'm adamant that there will not be children.

I won't be a mother. If you're counting on forever, if you're wanting a baby-making machine, you've got the wrong woman."

He leaned back in his chair, far more sympathetic to her situation than she knew. Like her, he'd never planned on marrying. He'd never wanted to father children. He'd long believed there were enough children in the world and he'd been determined never to add to the population boom.

"Children aren't at the top of my priority list right now," he answered calmly. "Sharif's son, Tahir, will inherit the throne on his twenty-fifth birthday, and his children from him. I am merely guardian of the throne until Tahir is of age."

"This is not a permanent arrangement, Zayed. This marriage is only temporary. You said so yourself earlier this morning."

"I said it'd be temporary if Sharif returns. If he doesn't..." His voice faded but not the meaning.

Rou shook her head fiercely, pink pearls swinging and clicking with her denial. "I won't spend the next twenty years with you while you wait for Tahir to grow up."

"It'd be twenty-three actually—"

"I'll give you a year."

"Ten."

Her eyebrows shot up. "Two."

"Nine."

"Nine years? Together? Are you mad?"

"No. I think I'm rather brilliant. You're perfect for me, and perfect as my queen. You can be an instrument of change here in Sarq. You could help reform our system, introduce laws to create more equality among the genders and make sure women are fully protected."

"You could do all that without me."

He suppressed a smile. "It wouldn't be as much fun."

"Fun? How can you even say that? You should be horrified at the idea of marrying me. I have your list somewhere, and I don't even meet half your desired attributes." Rou reached for her small bag, the pale pink croc clutch that Manar insisted she take with her, and pulled out a folded paper and smoothed it on the table. "Let's go over a few, shall we?"

He listened as she quoted back to him the traits he wanted, watching her face, the dark pink staining her cheeks, the bright fierce light in her eyes, the faintest quiver to her lower lip. When she finished, he lifted his hands. "But you are my list. You're exactly what I want. Smart, strong, confident, accomplished, compassionate."

But she shook her head, long pale hair tumbling over her shoulder. "No, you're wrong. I'm not the woman you want. I'm not a beautiful woman. I'm not noble. I'm not compassionate. If I accept, if I become your wife, it's because you can give me what I want."

She held her breath as though she'd said something very shocking, but he was intrigued, not troubled.

For Rou it was shocking because she was doing this, agreeing to this, because she benefited, not just

Zayed and his country. She would have the chance to be in Zayed's life, in Zayed's bed. She would have the chance to live out her fantasies, and then she'd be free to leave, to return to her career and her world of logic and reason. But at least she would have had this adventure, this chance to be someone else and experience what she had never felt.

Beauty. Hunger. Passion.

Aware that Zayed was watching her closely, she relaxed her clenched fist, smoothed the paper in front of her. "This isn't going to be a free ride for you, Zayed Fehr. You need a wife, any wife, and I'll be that wife, but there are conditions."

"I expected as much."

"Did you?" she shot back.

"Yes. Tell me."

"I want the research center. And the money," she said fiercely, lifting her chin and looking him in the eye.

"That will be expensive."

Dark rose stormed her cheeks, darkening her eyes so they looked like burning sapphires. "I will also continue working, and I will keep my name, keep my practice and keep my home in San Francisco."

He knew then, he'd kiss her again soon, very soon, if only to taste her soft, ripe mouth once more and feel that fierce spirit of hers. He'd never met a woman like her, and perhaps theirs wouldn't be a love match, but it would be passionate. He could guarantee that already.

"And what do I get again?" he asked softly.

"You get a wife." Her blue eyes shone. Her breasts rose and fell with every furious breath. "It's what you wanted." Her hard gaze met his and held, challenging him. "Wasn't it?"

CHAPTER SEVEN

ROU faced four pink evening gowns—a pale pink tulle; a mauve taffeta sparkly affair; a frothy, fuchsia ball gown; and a slinky, salmon silk—her choices for tonight's black-tie party, trying to decide on the lesser of the evils.

What a choice, and yet she had to make a choice. In just an hour she was to appear in the formal palace dining room for a prewedding dinner in her honor in one of these gowns. Having been briefed by Zayed, she knew that during the dinner she'd receive her engagement ring. She would also be introduced to all the family and friends that had been invited.

The wedding itself would take place late tomorrow morning, and then later in the evening in a much smaller ceremony Zayed would be crowned king.

But first, there was tonight's formal dinner to get through, a lavish party that could last late into the night with close to one hundred guests attending.

Queen Jesslyn and the children would be among the family members attending, and Zayed's younger brother, Sheikh Khalid Fehr, who'd been in the desert for the past several days as part of Sharif's rescue efforts. However, Khalid's young wife, Olivia, couldn't join them, although she'd sent word that she desperately wanted to be there, but being late in her pregnancy she couldn't fly. Zayed's mother wouldn't be there tonight, either, as she was still in the hospital, although she hoped to attend the wedding in the morning.

So many people. So many people there to look at her. Rou's stomach rose and fell in a sickly surge of panic. She didn't like being the center of attention, not like this. It was different when she was working, different when she was speaking, because she had a purpose then—she had a clear message to deliver—but tonight there was no message. Tonight her duty was to be attractive, groomed and agreeable.

Just like when she was a girl and dragged to court by her mother or father's attorney to testify against the other parent.

The attorneys always wanted her dressed up then, too. They all had an idea of how she should look, and she'd be forced to sleep in rollers to turn her straight hair into blond ringlets. They insisted on "pretty clothes"—frilly, pastel party dresses; white, lace-edged ankle socks; and shiny, black patent shoes. And dressed up like a living doll, she'd be marched into court and stared at and interrogated, photographed and pitied. Pity was the worst of all.

Eyes closing, Rou forced the hateful images away. It was long ago. She wasn't a child anymore. She wasn't helpless or powerless. She was a woman, and she'd agreed to help Zayed in order to help Sharif and his family.

She could do this. She just needed a dress. Just something less frilly to wear tonight.

A light knock sounded on the bedroom door and when Rou answered the door she found Zayed. "I brought you an alternative," he said, handing her a long, cream garment bag. "I didn't realize how much you hated pink."

She hesitated a moment before taking the garment bag. He was so big he seemed to fill the entire doorway. "And what is this? A peace offering in baby blue?" she answered mockingly, even as her fingers tingled and burned from where they'd brushed his.

"Close." His gaze held hers, the golden depths warm, and revealing amusement as he then gave her a shopping bag. "And these are the accessories. Shoes, jewelry, undergarments."

Her eyebrows arched as she struggled to ignore the coil of tension in her belly and how just that light brush of fingers made her back tingle and nipples harden. She was becoming far too sensitive around him, and far too responsive to the very real heat he generated whenever he looked at her. "Undergarments?"

"I thought you might want something special to wear under this gown."

"Did you buy them yourself or have one of your assistants do the shopping?"

"I did. The shop was near the hospital. It just made

sense." His smile turned crooked. "So if the sizes are off, you have no one but me to blame."

No one but him.

But wasn't that the problem? Her cool, logical, scientific mind had made the most hopeless of choices in falling for him.

Zayed wasn't safe. She wasn't going to leave Sarq without a broken heart, was she?

"I'm sure everything will fit fine," she said in a rush before thanking him and sending him out the door. But as she shut the door behind him, a hot flicker of pain shot through her, and she pressed a fist to her chest. It already hurt. Loving him would hurt.

Blinking back tears, Rou unzipped the cream garment bag to expose a featherlight gown the color of the sea, and felt her eyes sting. The dress was neither aqua nor cobalt, not turquoise or sapphire. It was a color so deep and intense and yet filled with light that she felt as though it'd been made just for her. Hand shaking, she drew the gown from the bag and the skirt tumbled to her feet in a long, narrow column of ocean blue with the softest, sheerest layer of chiffon over crushed silk.

Rou turned to the mirror, held the delicate gown against her chest and even in the soft light of her bedroom the fabric shimmered like water, like waves, and Rou, who'd never liked color before, loved this.

Rou, who'd never been beautiful, thought maybe, just maybe, tonight she would be beautiful. The very thought thrilled her, and she was ashamed at herself for being so shallow, but why couldn't she play the beautiful fairy princess just once? Why couldn't she pretend that she was one of those girls in the fairy tales who fell in love with a handsome prince and lived happily ever after?

Quickly she bathed so she could dress, and, still damp in her towel, she opened the shopping bag and took out the shoes and jewelry and undergarments which were just a small, silky pair of black panties. That was it.

Rou blushed and shook her head as she slid them on. The black panties were the softest silk, just wisps of fabric that covered next to nothing. But they were delicate and elegant and very sexy and the first sexy thing she'd ever owned.

Biting her lip, she looked at herself in the mirror in nothing but black panties against pale skin.

Definitely naughty. And pretty. And not pink.

The gown fit even better. It fit as though it was made for her, and she struggled with the zipper hidden in the side, but finally got it up so that she could turn to the mirror again. She loved what she saw. This was who she was. This is what she was. No frills, no bows, no puffy shoulders, nothing overtly girlie. The gown had one shoulder and it was an angular swathe of vivid chiffon. The bodice was narrow, pleated, and the skirt fell straight from beneath her ribs to her feet.

A mermaid, she thought with a shy, delighted smile at her reflection. Maybe beautiful women always felt this way looking at themselves, but for Rou, it was all so new. As she drew out the shoes, a strappy heel the color of bone, and then the accessories, thick, silver-and-diamond bangles for both wrists, and ornate, dangly, silver-and-diamond earrings for her ears, she felt giddy with excitement.

Tonight she vowed to enjoy herself. Tonight would be her night.

Manar knocked on her door. She'd come to check on Rou's progress and her smile of approval warmed Rou. "Beautiful," Manar said, inspecting Rou. "The color is like your eyes. Very beautiful."

"Thank you." Rou had never felt more beautiful but she put a hand self-consciously to her head. "What do you think I should do with my hair? Should I put it up, or leave it down? What would look best?"

Manar studied her another moment and then nodded decisively. "I will do it for you, yes?"

"Do you know how?"

Manar's smile broadened. "I am a ladies' maid in the palace. I have been trained to sew, do makeup, hair, nails, anything." She patted the low, pink uphol-stered chair before the dressing table. "Come sit, and I will show you."

Zayed stood in the arched corridor outside the vast dining room used for state occasions, greeting guests and making small talk as he waited for Rou to appear. She was late. Not by much, ten minutes, but it wasn't like her to run late, and he suddenly wondered if she'd heard the rumors about his past, about the curse hanging over his head, and she'd sneaked out of the palace and run away rather than face him.

He didn't blame her, if she had.

If he were her, he wouldn't marry himself. Everyone in Sarq knew that Prince Zayed Fehr was the dark prince, the doomed prince.

How ironic that he was here, then, in the palace, and Sharif was dead.

There was a rustle in the hall, and then she was rushing toward him, hands holding up the hem of her gown so she didn't trip. The circle of men around Zayed opened, scattered, allowing him to move forward to greet Rou.

Rich color stained her cheekbones. "I got lost!" she exclaimed low and breathlessly, reaching his side. "I told Manar I could find my way, but of course I turned the wrong way and then the wrong way again. The only other time I get this lost is in Manhattan, and I don't know why I lose my sense of direction in Manhattan."

She was mortified, he realized, discovering yet another little chink in her cool, logical armor, and it touched him, making him feel even more protective of her. "It's fine. You are the bride-to-be. You can keep us waiting as long as you like."

"No. Absolutely not. Punctuality is everything." She nodded for emphasis and her pale hair, strands both silver and gold, danced.

He'd never seen her with her hair in this style. It was pulled back from her brow, teased ever so slightly to form a blond crown above her forehead and then smoothed past her ears into a delicate knot at the back, where loose curls tumbled free.

It was a princess hairstyle, he thought, and in her shimmering, sea-blue gown, she looked like a sea princess, with her crown of silver-gold hair, and her pale, luminous skin gleaming against the gown's vivid silk.

"You look lovely," he said, and it was true. It was as if until now she'd kept herself shrouded in shadows and darkness, but suddenly the blinds were off and the lights flicked on and she shone from the inside out, beautiful, bold and brilliant.

"Thank you." Her smile was shy, and she lifted her wrists to show him the wide silver-and-diamond bracelets. "And dare I ask, are these real?"

"Yes."

"Real diamonds?" she persisted, jingling one ever so slightly. "Because I counted the diamonds. There are over fifty in each."

She was looking up at him, and her eyes matched her gown, rich, deep sea-blue, and he felt a rush of desire and possession. He wanted her, and the intensity of his desire caught him by surprise. He wanted her more than he'd wanted any woman in years. Perhaps more than anyone since Princess Nur. He hadn't allowed himself to think of her in so long that just her name, Nur, sent a shudder through him. Twenty-four-year-old Nur's violent death had been the beginning of the curse. He should have known better. He was seventeen, almost eighteen. He should have realized the consequences. Should have understood that the risks far outweighed the pleasure, but he'd been young, and so hopelessly in love.

"You must introduce me," a deep male voice spoke, and Zayed turned abruptly, gratefully, toward Khalid, his younger brother, hoping that interruption would put an end to memories of a past that had haunted him for nearly twenty years.

Khalid, like Zayed, was dressed in the formal ivory-and-gold robes of their country, although neither wore a head covering. In the palace, they never did. But as Zayed made the introductions, the past wouldn't fade; it was too alive tonight, bringing the loss and tragedy back with stunning force.

But then the past was never completely out of his mind. It stayed with him, the guilt weighing on him, eating away at any potential joy.

Yet he didn't want to forget, either. He owed Nur that much, and despite the party about to take place, and the beauty of his soon-to-be bride, he was living all over again the day he discovered she was dead.

He'd raged, how he'd raged, tearing through the palace, breaking things, shouting, screaming for justice, screaming her innocence, screaming his grief. It took all of his father's and brothers' and palace attendants' strength to keep young Zayed from going after Nur's husband. Zayed wanted revenge, needed revenge, but his family had locked him in the palace for months, until he was calmer and controlled, but getting there meant that he'd died, too. Nur's death had killed the boy and left the man—hard, strong, beautiful, and oh so empty. He was a man who had everything and yet nothing, and his curse stretched over the palace and the Fehr family.

First it claimed his sisters.

Then his father.

Now Sharif.

When would the tragedies end? When would something good begin?

Strains of music finally penetrated his brain, and Zayed came back to the present and the glow of candles and the loud hum of voices in the dining room. Next to him Khalid was talking to Rou, discussing one of her television appearances. Apparently he'd seen her once on *Oprah*, the American TV talk show, and Khalid was wondering if all American women needed so much relationship advice.

Of course Khalid and Rou would find it easy to converse. They were both scientists, although his area of study was archaeology and history, not psychology and anthropology.

Khalid and Rou were still talking when Zayed was given the signal that everyone was seated and ready for him to make his formal appearance in the dining room with Rou. Khalid then excused himself, going to sit with Jesslyn and the children, and the lights dimmed ever so slightly as musicians announced them.

"Ready?" Zayed asked her, looking down into her face, seeing a woman who deserved a far different life than the one she'd have now, a woman who deserved a far better man. But the only way he could do right by his family was by doing wrong to her.

Another tragedy.

Rou, who had been feeling unnaturally calm until this moment, looked up into the beautiful planes of Zayed's face and saw something so tortured and hollow in his gold eyes that her breath caught in her throat. He was sad, so very, very sad, and she knew suddenly that he wasn't anything close to the man she'd imagined him to be.

Realizing he was even more of a stranger than she'd thought, she felt a flurry of wild nerves, her pulse leaping maddeningly. Could she do this? Could she fulfill her promise to him?

Zayed, so handsome, so royal in his robes that her chest squeezed tight with the rush of emotion. She loved him.

She loved him?

Maybe she'd always loved him.

Rou took a quick breath, and then another, as she suddenly realized how much was at stake.

Her heart. Their happiness.

And now she had to walk into a room of one hundred people in a delicate gown that revealed more skin than she was accustomed to showing. Her soft, feminine hairstyle offered no protection, either. She had no crutch to use, no severe suit, no heavy glasses, nothing to protect her from others.

As if able to read her mind, Zayed took her arm, his voice deep. "I am with you. I will not leave your side. Not even if Sharif should walk through these doors."

He'd tried to be light, comforting, but the mention of Sharif brought a lump to her throat. "I wish he would walk through these doors."

She saw sorrow shade his eyes. "I do, too."

And then with her arm on his, they were moving through the grand dining room's enormous arched doors and into a large room with a soaring ceiling painted gold. The room itself gleamed with stunning precious metals, and Rou's heart pounded as they walked between long tables draped in heavy silk embroidered with glittering gold and silver thread. Extravagant, white floral arrangements covered the tables, as did hundreds, if not thousands, of glowing white candles.

The heady, sweet scent of the white lilies was overpowering, and in the soft gleam of candles, she felt dizzy, even dazed, as though she were a bride already.

Her heart pounded even harder as they approached the dais where they were to sit. It was raised above the room, just the way it might have been in a medieval castle. The lord and lady lifted above all.

Nervous, her fingers curled into Zayed's forearm, and she clung even more tightly to him. He was warm, and strong, steady and sure of himself. Thank God one of them was.

If this party weren't for them, if this evening's celebrations weren't for their betrothal, if this were for a friend or one of her clients, she'd be thinking it was glorious. She'd be thinking what a gorgeous party, what a perfect night. Only it was for her, for them, for their *wedding*, and the idea was so scary that despite Zayed's strong, steady arm, and despite his measured pace, she felt as though she were on a ship that was sinking. Any moment she would go under. Any moment now, she would drown.

She didn't drown during the three-hour dinner, at least, she hadn't yet, although her hand had shaken so badly when Zayed went to put on her engagement ring that she nearly knocked the ring from his hand.

Zayed had merely smiled as he grasped the ring more firmly and decisively slid it onto her finger. Rou's panic rose as the heavy ring settled onto her slim finger. She glanced down at it, thinking it felt more like a handcuff than a ring, but it was exquisite, an extremely large, rare blue diamond surrounded by chocolate and white diamonds. "It's not pink," she said with a shaky laugh.

His lips curved ruefully. "Your first ring was a pink diamond, but on hearing how much you hated pink, I thought a blue stone might suit you better."

Her heart sank at hearing that he'd gone to all the trouble to purchase a second ring, particularly when he had so many other matters to deal with. "I would have been happy with the pink one," she said softly, touching the blue oval diamond.

"Good. Because the pink one is still yours." He gestured to one of the attendants standing along the wall and the attendant returned with a jewel-encrusted mother-of-pearl box.

The sheikh took the box with the gold lock and small, gold, balled feet and opened it, revealing the pink diamond ring inside. "Consider it an early wedding gift. You may choose to wear it as a cocktail ring, or you may sell it. It's yours."

The ring inside was stunning, but it came nowhere near the splendid design of the mother-of-pearl and ruby jewelry box that caught the candlelight and reflected it like fire. "This is gorgeous," she whispered, reverently turning the box this way and that. "Is it an antique?"

"It dates to 1534 and was designed by Pierre Mangot. It was a gift for the French king, Francis I."

She tried to press it back into Zayed's hands. "It's too costly a gift—"

"Nonsense. In Sarq, the groom always showers the bride with extravagant gifts, and even if we were not here in Sarq, I would still be compelled to give you beautiful things. You are a beautiful woman. You deserve nothing less."

Zayed's words stayed with her the rest of the night, and she heard them repeat as he walked her back to her wing at one-thirty in the morning.

Zayed was quiet as they walked, and her nerves were wound so tight that she could barely breathe.

Tomorrow they'd marry.

Tomorrow she'd probably go with him to his room.

It was what she wanted, but her desires also filled her with fear. She wasn't experienced enough…hadn't dated enough…hadn't been with enough men to approach sex with anything like calm or composure.

Suddenly Rou just wanted to be in her room and alone. She wanted to hide. Wanted to return to her self, her real self, the plain woman with the sober wardrobe and severe hairstyle.

She wanted the safe Rou, the predictable one, not this dress-up princess that wore elegant heels and delicate gowns and silver-and-diamond earrings on her earlobes.

But maybe Sharif would still return in time. Maybe he'd walk through the doors tomorrow morning saving them all from a dreadful mistake.

It would be a mistake, too.

Darting a glance at Zayed from the corner of her eye confirmed her worst fears. He was the most beautiful man she'd ever seen. He was beyond physical perfection. How could she trust a man like him? He had everything a man could want, everything a man could need. How could he, how would he, ever be content with her?

How could a man like that ever love a woman like her?

He might be intrigued, might see her as a challenge, or a conquest, but it'd never be love. He himself said he didn't know how to love….

She was practically trembling in her shoes by the time they turned down the corridor that led to her wing, and as she spotted the now-familiar stonework that led to her sunken living room, she felt pure relief. Soon she'd be in her own pajamas, in bed, and at least for one night, away from Zayed and this terrible, oppressive sense of doom.

But once in her living room Zayed was in no hurry to leave. He wandered around the dimly lit room touching this and that before opening the French doors onto the moonlit garden, allowing them to hear the light, tinkling splash of the courtyard fountain.

Rou watched him stand in the doorway, drinking in the cool night air. The moonlight dappled his face light and dark. "Do you have any questions about tomorrow?" he asked, his deep voice unusually rough.

"No."

He turned around to face her. "You understand the expectations? The morning ceremony and then the afternoon together…?"

She moved farther from him, retreating to the low white couches where she kicked off her shoes and sat down on one, her legs curling beneath her. "I believe so."

"We must consummate the marriage for it to be valid."

Her heart raced and her stomach knotted, screaming in protest. "We couldn't just tell everyone we did the deed?" she choked.

He leaned against the open door frame, his mouth compressing, his expression strangely brooding for such a celebratory night. "Can't lie. Karma and all."

"How would such a little lie bring the wrath of the gods?"

He drew a fist across his mouth. "Little lies do," he said, his voice so deep and hoarse Rou felt it scratch across her heart.

Afraid, but not sure why, she wrapped a protective

arm around her legs. "You sound as if you speak from experience, my prince," she said shakily, wondering at the tension coiling in the room.

Zayed closed his eyes briefly before looking at her, and yet even once he did look at her, he didn't really seem to see her. No, he seemed to be somewhere else, seeing something—or someone—else. "Little lies are the worst. Those are the ones that appear so innocent, so foolish as to be silly, but the little lies are the ones that will break you. They're the ones that will cut you, stealing your soul."

He rubbed his fist across his mouth, eyes so dark with memories that they were nearly as black as the night outside. "In marrying you, I am pledging to you my fidelity, my respect and my protection. While we're married, while together, I will never take another. You will be my only wife, and my only woman. And I mean that with every breath that I take, with every breath that I am."

Rou sat very still as his words sank into her. She could feel truth and anger in the promise he made her, and she felt a lick of fear, wondering how everything had gotten so intense so quickly. They were back to emotions, very deep, very dark emotions, and this was definitely out of her comfort zone. But then everything here in Sarq was out of her comfort zone.

"You make me realize I do not even know you," she said unsteadily, hugging her legs. "You seem so much the playboy, but I'm beginning to think that you're nothing like a playboy…nothing like the image you've projected all these years."

He laughed grimly. "Do not imagine me a hero. I am not Sharif, or Khalid, nor will I ever be."

"Then who are you?"

He left the door and walked slowly, deliberately toward her. He was still so graceful, and yet his focus had an almost lethal quality. "The family shame," he answered, reaching her side and towering above her.

Rou's pulse quickened, and she had to tip her head back to see his face. "You are by far the most beautiful and financially successful of your brothers. How can beauty and wealth be a source of shame?"

He traced her profile, his finger lightly covering her brow, the length of her nose, the curve of lips and then chin. "Oh you of all people should know that beauty and wealth are deceitful gifts. Some of the world's most evil men have hidden their true nature behind beautiful faces."

Her skin flushed and burned beneath his light touch. "Are you evil, Zayed?"

He reached down and pulled her into his arms and lifted her to her feet, bringing her so close that she could feel the hard length of his body from his chest to his knees. "No," he murmured against her cheek, his warm breath tingling her ear. "But I am cursed."

Rou shivered against him. "Do not say such things."

He wrapped an arm snugly around her waist, holding her in such a way that she could feel the size of his ribs, the lean hips, hard thighs, as well as the rigid male length between. "But I have promised to protect you," he said, his lips trailing ever so slowly across her cheek to the edge of her mouth, "and that includes protecting you from me."

And then he tilted her head back, and his lips covered hers, hungry and fierce, as if a man starved. She felt her own mouth tremble beneath the pressure of his, even as a terrible weakness filled her belly. She felt weak and empty and in desperate need of his arm holding her up, holding her against him, holding her as though he never intended to let her go.

Zayed kissed her thoroughly, parting her lips, taking her mouth, taking her tongue between his lips, kissing her until she shivered and shuddered, burning from the inside out. With veins hot and thick, veins that felt as though they were filled with stinging honey, Rou lost all track of time, lost track of everything but this fierce fire between them.

Long minutes later when Zayed lifted his head, he stroked her flushed cheek, as if marveling at its softness. "You are too good, too innocent, for a life with me, *laeela*," he said regretfully, "but I cannot ignore duty. Not now, not after all these years. I have to honor Sharif, and that means I have to have you."

CHAPTER EIGHT

Rou slept fitfully, waking every hour from vivid, intense dreams. Zayed featured prominently in every one, and Rou didn't know if it was the kiss or her feverish imagination, but she woke up afraid, terribly aware that today everything changed.

Today she became vulnerable. She married the man she loved, and yet he didn't love her back. And she'd found what it was her clients all wanted, only for her, the wedding and marriage were just temporary.

Agitated, she turned on her side, her arm as her pillow, and she looked out the small, high window that showed the sky. It wasn't dawn yet but the sky was lighter, the dark blue night sky giving way to a layer of light blue. Somewhere the sun was already up. Soon it'd be up here, too. Soon she'd be Zayed's wife.

Her eyes closed, lashes fluttering against her cheek as she drew a frightened breath.

She didn't know how to do this. Didn't know how to become any man's, not even his.

It wasn't just consummating the marriage that filled her with anxiety, although that was terrifying in and of itself. At least she wasn't completely in-experienced. She'd had sex a couple times many years ago, but it'd felt wrong—it'd hurt—and the doctor in her knew it was a combination of emotional and physical pain. She didn't love either of the men, and she wasn't properly aroused, which contributed to her discomfort. But her fear today was different. Her fear was disappointing Zayed. He'd called her beautiful, called her passionate, but what would he say when he discovered she was useless, ridiculous in bed?

Sharif had once asked her why she didn't date more, and she'd answered that her work consumed her, but it hadn't always just been about her work. In her midtwenties when she'd tried dating, she'd discovered she was hopeless at it. Everybody wanted casual sex. She couldn't have casual sex. And those two times a relationship developed sufficiently that she thought she should try to have a physical relationship, it went wrong, so wrong. Sex itself felt invasive. A man on top of you, surrounding you, filling you.

But later today it wouldn't be just anyone with her. Today it would be Zayed.

Her stomach lurched, and she threw back the covers and swung her legs from the bed.

Calm down, she told herself, going to the living room to the French doors and opening them to welcome in the cool, sweet air. He might be disappointed, but he'll have done his duty and you'll both survive.

* * *

Manar arrived early with breakfast and coffee and elaborate plans to help Rou prepare for her ceremony. "In my country we henna the bride's hands and feet," she said, smiling as she poured Rou's coffee and served her a selection of flaky pastries from the tray. "I think you would find it wonderful and unusual."

Rou gratefully sipped her strong coffee. "You're not from Sarq?"

The maid shook her head. "I am from Baraka, a country not far, and while not terribly different, we do celebrate marriage differently."

"How did you get to Sarq?"

Manar smiled, dimpling. "My husband. He is one of Prince Khalid's men, and I met him while he accompanied the prince to Baraka on business."

"Do you return home often?"

The maid shook her head. "It is too far and quite costly to travel."

"Don't you miss your family?"

She shrugged. "I would miss my husband more if I was not with him."

Jesslyn appeared in the arched doorway. "Am I interrupting?" she asked.

"No, not at all. Please come in, Your Highness." Rou rose and went to greet Jesslyn with a kiss on each cheek. "How are you?"

"Excited for you."

A lump filled Rou's throat. Jesslyn was so good and kind. "Thank you."

"I have brought you a gift for your wedding day,"

the queen added, holding out a small, tissue-wrapped package. "Every bride must have something borrowed, something blue, and this is both. I thought perhaps you could tuck it inside the strap of your bodice, or maybe your purse."

Rou sat and opened the small gift. It was a fine white handkerchief embroidered with an elaborate S and F in dark blue thread.

"It was Sharif's," Jesslyn said with an uncertain smile. "He was quite a fan of yours and I thought this would be a way to include him. It's borrowed, and it's kind of blue."

Rou clutched the handkerchief in her hand, the square of starched fabric more precious than Jesslyn knew. "You will make me cry."

Jesslyn's eyes were already pink with tears. "He'd be so happy for you and Zayed. He loved both of you and the fact that you have found each other..." She shook her head, her voice drifting off. "I'm sorry. I promised I wouldn't break down. I don't want to be sad, and I don't want to make you sad on your special day."

Rou reached out and took Jesslyn's hand. "You've made it special, Your Highness—"

"Jesslyn, please. We are to be sisters. And friends, I hope."

Rou squeezed her hand gently. "Yes. With all my heart."

Jesslyn leaned forward and gave Rou a swift hug and then rose. "I won't keep you. I know you're busy. But know you can come to me for anything, and—" She broke off, hesitating, dark brows tugging together in consternation. "And don't listen to rumors. The palace is full of them, especially when it comes to Zayed. He's a bit of a mystery around here and there are many staff members who don't really understand him. He certainly isn't cursed, no matter what they say."

Cursed.

That word again, and this time from Jesslyn herself.

Rou's mouth went dry, and she reached for her glass of guava juice and took a small sip. "People can be ignorant, can't they?"

Jesslyn nodded. "They can be, and it's so unfair. He was so young, just a boy, and hopelessly romantic. If he committed a crime, it was of being naive, and yet the consequences were so severe, so vile it's more than the mind can take in." Her expression softened. "Sharif has worried about him for years, and so to see Zayed here, now, taking his place as the head of the family, is bittersweet. Bitter, because Sharif isn't here, but sweet because Zayed deserves so much more than he's known."

And then Jesslyn was kissing her cheek and hurrying out the door, leaving Rou even more conflicted than she'd been before.

So there was a curse. And something terrible had happened. Zayed had suffered, as did the family. But why? What had happened?

Manar appeared with towels on her arm. "My lady,

I've drawn your bath. It's time for you to begin preparing for your wedding. The ceremony is in less than two hours."

The ceremony was short and simple, neither religious nor sentimental. She and Zayed stood next to each other in the palace reception room for the exchange of vows and rings. It was essentially a civil ceremony with fifteen witnesses, immediate family and a few visiting heads of state, with the rest of the guests to join them later for the luncheon.

Zayed had surprised her with another dress, this one for the wedding. He hadn't brought it to her personally, but one of the palace staff carried it to her room and it was perfect. The long silver-gray skirt had a fitted matching top with snug three-quarter sleeves. The glamorous yet understated design reminded Rou of Hollywood fashions in the 1940s, and Manar knew exactly what to do with Rou's hair, twisting and putting it up like a 1940s pinup.

Her only jewelry was her wedding ring and her own simple pearl stud earrings, but it was enough, and now with the service concluding, and the Sarq Minister of Justice giving them the traditional Sarq blessing, it was over.

They were married.

She darted a nervous glance at Zayed as they turned to face their guests. He looked so calm, so strong, and she wondered at his composure in light of what he had said last night.

What was this curse hanging over his head? And what had he done to bring such shame to his family? It must have been significant for palace staff to still gossip about it so many years later.

His gaze caught hers, and he smiled faintly, but there was no time for words as they were being swarmed by Jesslyn and Sharif's children eager to give their uncle and new aunt hugs and kisses.

The greetings and congratulations continued through lunch. Close to seventy attended, with many international names and faces, including a former American president, an ex-British prime minister, and a host of royal figureheads along with some of the region's most powerful men, like the Sultan of Baraka, Malik Nuri; Nuri's younger brother, Kalen; and their friend and neighbor, the desert chieftain, Sheikh Tair.

Sitting at the head table, Rou's gaze drifted around the room, puzzling a little over the number of powerful men in attendance, men without their wives.

"What's the matter?" Zayed asked, leaning toward her to whisper in her ear.

"All these men…they're so famous, and powerful. Aren't they all heads of state?"

"Most, yes."

She gave her head a shake. "But why are their wives not here? Why are they here alone?"

"They've come for the coronation and the wedding, but the coronation is for men only." Zayed looked into her eyes. "But you knew that, right?"

"No." She frowned and then ducked her head. "Am I not allowed to be there, either?"

"No, *laeela*. I am sorry."

"Ah." She looked up, managed a smile. "It's probably quite boring."

His gaze held hers. "Sometimes the laws are very archaic. I am sorry."

"It doesn't matter." But she could see from the sympathy in his eyes that he knew she was disappointed. "Don't look at me like that," she whispered. "I don't want to be emotional here, not in front of everyone."

His lips curved, his long black lashes dropping to conceal his deep gold eyes, eyes that always seemed to see too much. "I like your fiery side. When you're passionate, your eyes blaze and your lips tighten and you become so very righteous. It's exciting."

Under the tablecloth she slipped her foot on top of his and pressed down, pinching his foot beneath hers. He let out a little oath and looked at her, surprised, and she lifted her eyebrows. "Let that be a warning. You don't want to provoke me."

He grinned, showing off a rare dimple deep in his cheek. "I have a suspicion that you are all ice on the outside, but all fire underneath."

She opened her mouth to protest but couldn't, not when he looked into her eyes like that, looking so long, so deep that her pulse leaped and her head swam. No one ever looked at her the way Zayed did. He looked with interest, with curiosity, with hunger.

Hunger.

Her face flooded with warmth, the same warmth coursing through her veins, a tingling that started in her belly and radiated out making her skin sensitive and her nerves dance.

His dark head tipped near hers. "I look forward to when we're finally alone," he said, his voice so low that no one could possibly hear but her.

Air caught in her throat. Her fingers curled into her palms, her enormous blue diamond wedding ring heavy and still so new on her hand.

"It won't be long now," he added, "an hour at the most. And don't worry, I will take it slow. There is nothing to fear."

Embarrassed, she lifted her chin and whispered fiercely, "I'm not afraid. It's not my first time."

"You're not a virgin?"

She could feel the heat in her cheeks, her eyes just as overbright. "I'm thirty years old."

His lips tugged, and it appeared as though he were trying very hard not to smile. "I will still take my time. I promise to make it pleasurable for both of us."

Zayed's gaze rested on her face, enchanted by the vivid wash of rose in her cheeks. It'd been a long time since he met a woman that blushed.

"You don't have to drag it out," she said, lips compressing. "We have a job to do. Let's just get it done."

"Is that how you view lovemaking?"

She gave him a sharp look and muttered, "We're not in love, therefore it's not lovemaking."

"Is there a more scientific name you prefer?"

He could see her mind race, considering all the different possibilities, and none of them pleased her. Her mouth compressed even smaller, her chin set. "To call it sex is fine."

And Zayed, who had so much on his mind, and so much pain in his heart, felt something else in his heart, and it wasn't sorrow or grief, but a lightness that hadn't been there in weeks.

My God she was funny. And nervous. And tongue-tied.

And perfect. Perfectly prickly. Perfectly priceless.

An hour later they'd said their goodbyes to their guests and were excused from the after party and now were in Zayed's wing. His suite of rooms and the furnishings were bold and royal and utterly magnificent. Rou stood in the middle of his living room, noting how his plaster walls were draped with regal tapestries and the low couches and drapes were all rich midnight-blue velvets and silks embroidered with gold.

Turning her head, she saw an open doorway, and through that she glimpsed an enormous bed, this, too, covered in rich blue velvet. She looked away, wishing she hadn't seen it, knowing exactly what would happen in there in just a matter of time.

"A glass of champagne?" he asked, reaching for a bottle chilling in a silver ice bucket.

She hadn't had anything to drink at lunch—only half the guests drank due to culture and religion—but a glass of champagne sounded perfect now. It might even take away that terrible bite of nerves. "Please," she said, pressing a hand to her stomach as if she could quiet the butterflies.

"Do sit," he said, as he expertly popped the cork.

She looked around for a safe spot to sit and chose the only single chair in the room. Zayed smiled as he noted her choice of seating, which only made her sit taller and straighter on the low velvet chair.

He filled two crystal flutes, carried them to her and handed one over.

"Cheers," she said quickly, brightly.

He looked down into her eyes. "To a long and happy marriage."

She flushed and winced, thinking his toast made hers sound shallow and insincere. "To a long and happy marriage," she answered more quietly, clinking the rim of her flute to his. The crystal tinged and then she drank, letting the cold, dry champagne bubble across her tongue and fizz all the way down as she swallowed. The cold bubbles brought tears to her eyes and warmth to her middle. "This is good."

"You don't usually drink," he said, taking a seat on the blue velvet couch across from her and stretching his arm along the back. He looked so comfortable, so at ease with himself and life that she felt a burst of envy. Life would be so different if she behaved as he did—owning his space, seizing it, taking as much as life offered. Unlike her, who tried to take as little as possible.

She took another quick sip. "Not much, no."

"Why?"

"This is your inheritance," she said, lifting a hand to gesture around the palatial suite. "Mine is a little different."

His gaze narrowed. "Was it your mother or father who drank?"

"My father." She felt her cheeks warm. "My mother preferred pills."

His gaze rested on her flushed face. "Not you?"

"No. I'm an adult child of addicts. I have other issues. Lack of trust. Problems with boundaries. Serious need for control." Her lips curved, self-mocking. "I'm sure none of this is news to you, though. You've spent enough time studying me."

"You never talk about your parents."

Her chin lifted. "I just did."

"Your parents were very famous."

"And famous for their lack of control." She took another long sip from her champagne, her flute now half-empty, and then resolutely set the glass on the low table between them.

His gaze never left her face. "Why do you hide your beauty? You're as beautiful, if not more beautiful, than your mother, and she was one of the great beauties of her time."

It was all Rou could do to stay seated. She longed to leap up and move. Pace. Walk. Run.

Run away.

Instead she swallowed the panic rushing through her, panic stirred by memory and painful emotions, and forced herself to answer calmly, "Beauty means nothing if it's selfish. Hurtful."

"You are neither."

"Because I've chosen not to focus on the externals. I've committed my life to finding true beauty, inner beauty. It's why I work to help people find true companionability, relationships built on shared values and needs."

He said nothing for a moment, intent on listening, watching. Finally, "If I had gone through your matchmaking system, what would have happened, after the first meet?"

She shrugged. "Second dates, third dates…eventually love."

"Pippa told me you had rules for the dates, including rules about sex."

"I think you have sex on the brain," she said tartly, pressing her hands together to keep from making wild, nervous gestures.

He laughed, creases fanning from his eyes. "I'd be lying if I said I didn't. You are incredibly beautiful, as well as intriguing. Does it bother you that I look forward to being with you?"

Rou swallowed hard and, crossing her legs, turned the conversation back to her matchmaking rules. "Pippa was right. I do discourage my clients from sleeping together for the first five meets. After that, it's up to them."

"But why five dates, and why the need for any rules at all?"

"Sex changes the relationship, particularly for women. The majority of women feel emotionally involved from the point they make love. Men don't internalize sex the same way. Abstinence levels the playing field."

She thought he'd laugh, but instead his expression sobered. "Do you think sex will change the way you feel about me?" he asked quietly.

She opened her mouth, then shut it. "I…I don't know. I doubt it."

"Why?"

"I haven't ever felt close to a man after sex." There, she'd said it. She shrugged a little to hide her discomfort and waited for him to say something, but he didn't. He just regarded her with those intense gold eyes.

"I'm probably not the most experienced woman alive," she continued, "but at the same time, I know enough to know how I respond…and…" Suddenly her courage was gone. She couldn't find the words to say that she didn't respond, that in bed, she didn't feel. It was her own failure as a woman, and one she'd decided not to focus on as there were so many things she could do. But now that failing loomed large, and she was terrified of not just disappointing herself, again, but of disappointing him.

"Do you always sleep with a woman on a first date?" she asked abruptly.

"Do I always?" He appeared puzzled. "I rarely sleep with a woman on a first date. It's not my thing."

"Why? Men want sex—"

"And so do women, but it's almost always better when you know someone a little bit, don't you think?" He rose from his couch and crossed to where she sat. He surprised her by lifting her from her chair, taking her seat on the chair and then drawing her down onto his lap.

"There, that's better," he said. "It's hard to talk about sex across the room from you."

Rou stiffened, giving him her profile as she stared uncomfortably across the handsome room. His lap was hard beneath her thighs, and his body's warmth penetrated the thin, silver organza skirt.

He laughed softly at her expression. "What's wrong?"

"It's—" she glanced at him from beneath her lashes "—awfully close."

She felt rather than heard the laughter rumbling in his chest.

"It's going to get closer, *laeela*," he answered gravely, and yet she saw the warm gleam in his eyes, that look he gave her when he was fully aware and fully engaged.

He was enjoying himself. Her heart gave a lurch, and she knotted her hands into fists to try to stop them from shaking. "Perhaps we should just do it quickly," she suggested breathlessly. "Get it over with so we can get on with the day."

She felt the laughter rumble through him again, up through his broad chest and into his eyes and mouth. He was always gorgeous, so beautifully put together, but with the laughter warming his eyes and playing on his lips, he looked like an angel among mortals. How was a woman to resist such a man? Rou couldn't tear her eyes from his face. It wasn't fair that any man had such a face. It was a face that left even her weak. Her fingers itched to explore the striking planes and hollows. Those cheekbones, the straight slash of nose, and that mouth of his with the upper lip that curved so wickedly, so sensually promising, promising…

"Your expression is priceless," he murmured as she continued her slow study.

She looked up into his eyes. "Is it?"

"Mmm. You look as if you can't decide if you love me or loathe me."

Blood rushed to her face. "I can assure you, it's loathe, Your Highness."

He had the gall to laugh.

CHAPTER NINE

His laughter gave way to a smile he was trying very hard to suppress, and yet his eyes glinted, and his wicked mouth curved. "You say that with your lips, *laeela*, but your body says something else."

She sat even straighter, trying to minimize the areas where their legs touched. "*My* body does?"

"Mmm." He stroked down her back, once, and again. "Your body likes being near me, and I very much like your body near mine."

"You're mistaken."

"Am I?" He turned her ever so slightly on his lap so that she faced him more fully, and more of her legs dangled over his, and now her shoulder pressed to his chest.

She felt the pulse at the base of her neck flutter. "Yes."

He just smiled and, watching her face, he slid his hand along the curve of her jaw, toward her ear and up into her hair. Rou's toes nearly curled with pleasure. It wasn't the most sexual touch and yet it both stirred and soothed her, making her want to stretch and luxuriate beneath his touch. He rubbed her nape for a few moments, his fingers working against her scalp and this was pure pleasure. Eyes half closing, she was so tempted to give in to the sensation, so tempted to just lean against him and relax.

But Rou never leaned against anyone, never leaned on anyone, either. She meant what she'd said—she had issues with trust and control, and the last person she could trust was this man. Even if he was now her husband.

But Zayed was in no hurry, and he seemed to enjoy touching her as much as she enjoyed being touched. After a while he stroked down her neck and massaged a little at her shoulders, and then a little deeper so that her knotted muscles eased and her tension began to dissipate. If he noticed that she sat less rigidly in his arms, he gave no indication, focused as he was on making her relax.

And she was relaxing. A little voice in the back of her brain was lecturing her that she was practically purring, but Rou wasn't very interested in listening to the little voice right now.

It felt so good to be touched. To be massaged like this. She felt spoiled, decadent, like a big cat soaking up the sun.

As one of his hands caressed the length of her spine, the other began plucking the pins from her hair, pulling the silver sticks out one by one until her hair fell free, tumbling to her shoulders.

He wasn't content with that, though. He drew his

hand through the smooth length, pulling it apart so that her pale hair tangled and spilled in wild disorder down her back. With her hair now loose, he drew back to look at her, his gaze traveling slowly, deliberately over her face, her eyes, her nose, her mouth. "You are a remarkably beautiful woman, Princess Fehr."

She arched an eyebrow, her heart hammering like mad. "Princess?"

"You are my wife, my consort, and later tonight you will be my queen."

She didn't know if it was his body heat penetrating hers, or the slow caress of his hand, but she felt dazed, drugged, her thoughts slow. "I can't think of anyone less royal than me."

He dragged his hands through her hair, tugging her head back to expose her throat. "Then you should see yourself through my eyes." He lowered his head to her throat and kissed her just beneath her jaw on skin that suddenly felt so very, very sensitive. He kissed farther back on the pulse leaping beneath her earlobe, and then tugged with his teeth on the lobe itself sending sparks of fire through her body. Rou bit the inside of her lip to keep from making a sound.

His hands circled the base of her exposed throat and caressed up to her chin, his thumbs discovering nerve endings she didn't even know she had. When he reversed direction to stroke down she nearly leaped out of her skin at how exquisitely sensitive she'd become. It was as if each stroke of his fingers was heightening the tension, and the pleasure.

"You're awfully good at this," she choked, as his mouth pressed fleeting kisses to little invisible nerves along her neck and jaw. Yet those nerves were definitely tied to nerves elsewhere as her spine arched and her belly ached, hot and tight and throbbing for something she knew not.

"You have a deliciously responsive body," he answered before gently biting at the muscle that ran along her shoulder.

Rou gasped, shivered.

He blew on the hair at her nape and she jerked in his arms, her body no longer under her control but his. "You're sure?" she gasped again.

She could feel his smile against her neck. "Mmm, quite sure," he answered, his voice deep, husky. And then as he kissed the back of her neck, his hands were on the small buttons at the back of her top, and one by one he undid the little pearls until he could slide the snug fabric from her shoulders and down onto her arms before pulling it from her body.

She felt naked in her bra and she turned against his chest, hiding her face in the hollow between his shoulder and neck.

"Don't be shy," he murmured.

"I can't help it."

"Then let me help." And he turned her on his lap, so that she faced away from him. And with her back before him, he lifted her hair, and kissed his way down her spine, kissing each vertebra until he reached her bra and then deftly he unhooked that, too, pushing the straps over her shoulders and off her arms so that the air rushed at her bare skin, puckering her breasts that already felt strangely heavy, strangely not hers.

She wanted something from him, something that would answer the drumming in her veins, but she didn't know what it was. More kisses? More touch? More what?

And then his hands slid round to cup her breasts, and she closed her eyes, shocked by the sensation. Her body didn't feel like her body. Her body didn't feel like anything she'd ever known before, and with eyes closed, she focused on the new, seductive pleasure. He stroked beneath her breasts, stroked the soft, full sides, and, lips parting, she found herself arching into his hands, arching into what he could give her.

And he gave to her, alternately stroking and tugging on the heavy ripeness, drawing heat and fire from deep inside to every inch of exposed skin. Her hard nipples tightened again into taut, aching peaks, and she gritted her teeth helplessly, wanting more of everything, especially pressure, friction, sensation.

Lifting from beneath her breasts, thumbs pinching her nipples, he arched her the other way, back toward him, her body helplessly curving to his will, his arousal hard between her thighs.

His powerful thighs shifted, knees widening to part her legs so that she rested more fully on his erection. He was hard, so hard and warm, and the heat and friction were a new torment.

Ruthlessly Rou bit into her lower lip as he rocked

her against him, the tip of his thick shaft sliding back and forth against the sensitive area between her thighs. It was wanton, it was shocking, it was maddening, and she couldn't have asked him to stop even if she wanted him to. This was pleasure beyond anything she'd ever known, and somehow it was right with him, somehow she'd known it would be this way—darkly sensual, mind-blowingly erotic.

His hands slid down to her hips where he found the zipper of her skirt and with a quick unzip, a tug and a lift, the skirt was off her legs and he was resettling her on his lap, but parting her thighs wider, bringing her even lower, harder on his erection so that she could feel the length of him. There was a lot of him to feel. Her scrap of silk panties were of no use as she just grew hotter, wetter, more aroused.

With an arm beneath her breasts, he held her to him, and stroked her with the other hand, first over the delicate damp silk, and then when she was clenching her jaw, groaning at the pleasure, beneath the edge of silk, his fingers tracing the delicate folds and inner folds and then the tight highly sensitized bud between. One flick of his finger there and she bucked wildly. Another stroke and she felt her eyes burn, her body dancing for him to touch her, take her, possess her.

By the time he slipped a finger inside her she was desperate for him, all of him. Reaching backward she grabbed his hips, and ground down onto his lap. "You better finish what you started," she panted, "and quickly, before I lose it completely."

With a rumble in his chest he shifted her off him, dispensed with his shoes, socks, shirt and pants in no time and then she was back down on his lap, but facing him. Rou panicked, though, pushing her hands against his chest. "I can't do it this way," she said, "can't be on top—"

"Yes, you can. And you can look at me, because you need to see what you do to me." And then, cupping her face in his hands, he kissed her, deeply, fiercely, taking her mouth and tongue as though they were his, and in a way, they were. She knew somewhere inside her that a very real part of her belonged to him, had always belonged to him and that was why she'd been so afraid. She was afraid of this power he had over her, and he did have a power. Just look at her. She was putty in his hands.

And, kissing her, he lifted her up, and drew her slowly, so very slowly down on his hard, thick length. Rou exhaled in a quick puff, shocked by his size and the sense of fullness and invasion. He was stretching her, opening her and it stunned her body as much as it stung her heart. She wasn't used to being shared, wasn't used to being part of anyone else.

"Easy, baby," he murmured against her mouth, hands beneath her bottom, supporting her weight until she could relax again and better accommodate him.

But she shook her head and wrapped her arms around his shoulders and buried her face against him. "I can't, I can't, I can't. I don't know how to do this, don't know how to feel this."

"It's just me, *laeela*."

She squeezed her eyes more tightly shut. "That's what I'm afraid of."

"You're afraid of me?"

Despite her panic she heard the hesitation in his voice, and the shadow of sadness. Tears seeped from beneath her lashes. The last thing she wanted to do was hurt him. "Not of you. Just afraid to love you."

He didn't move. She wasn't even sure he was breathing.

"Someone has to love me," he said after an endless moment.

Rou's heart convulsed and the tears she'd been fighting fell. Lifting her head she looked into his eyes. He was so beautiful, and the expression in his eyes was so alone, so alone and lonely, and yet here they were, naked, pressed flesh to flesh.

Her lower lip trembled. "Let me try then," she said, fresh tears falling. "Let me be the one to try." And then she clasped his face in her hands and kissed him, kissing him the way he'd kissed her, deeply, hungrily, desperately.

He, this beautiful man, needed her, and she needed him and her heart cracked open to let him all the way in, to allow her to feel something other than fear. And as her heart opened, her body opened for him, too, taking him inside her, joining them, making them one.

She didn't ride him, but instead they moved together, his hands on her hips, her lips clinging to his. She buried her fingers into his hair, her breasts crushed to his chest as the friction became a bitter-sweet sensation and then a maddening tension. The pleasure grew, intensified, the sensation of their bodies became everything. She felt her heart drumming, felt her body glow hot, felt every nerve ending from her toes to her head tighten. Her nerves and senses focused, and her mind closed to everything but the intense pressure building, ruthless, relentless, until there was nothing she could do but explode in a firestorm of feeling.

Dimly she was aware of Zayed's body tensing and thrusting hard and deep into her. Dimly she felt his release. Dimly, because she'd never felt anything like this orgasm before, had never even climaxed before, and it was unbelievable, indescribable.

Exhausted, she leaned weakly against him, their bodies warm and damp, hers still quivering with aftershocks.

They sat there like that for several minutes, until Zayed lifted her off and into his arms and carried her into the bedroom where he pulled back the covers and put her down in the cool, smooth sheets and then lay down beside her.

"What now?" she asked.

He wrapped an arm around her and drew her against him. "Sleep," he answered gruffly. He did, and after several minutes, she did, too.

Rou didn't know how long she slept in the cool, dark room, but when she finally woke, she was alone. Padding to the door, she peeked into the living room. It was empty, their clothes now folded and neatly stacked on the table between the couches. She then headed for the ensuite bath to see if he was there.

The bathroom was empty, but she could still feel the humid warmth and smell a whiff of lingering aftershave. It was subtle but spicy, and it filled her with the strangest feeling—tenderness mixed with lust. She glanced around, noting the used towels hanging from a hook on the door, and the wet mat in front of the large marble-and-glass shower. He'd showered, shaved and gone.

Duty fulfilled, she thought sardonically, he was now free to become king.

And even though she knew she was being petty, it still hurt inside her. She'd enjoyed what had happened between them, and yet she was also a little shocked by it. By her. She'd wanted him, wanted it all, and he'd answered her need beyond a doubt.

But now, alone, she felt empty. And scared. When they'd made love, she'd given him more than her body, she'd given him her heart.

He could hurt her now. It'd be so easy to hurt her now.

Turning, she caught movement in the mirror and stared at the woman in the mirror, perplexed. Who was that blonde? Who looked like that? All lips and blue eyes, all softness and passion, fire and need?

She looked at herself long and hard and then with a sinking heart, whispered, "It's me."

But her vulnerability scared her; her softness threatened her, and, climbing into the shower, Rou turned the water on full force, as cold as she could take it, and washed her hair, and ruthlessly washed her body, particularly the tender skin between her legs. Her teeth chattered by the time she'd finished showering but she'd done the job. She'd chased away the warmth and tenderness, chilled the passion and need.

Stepping out of the shower, she wrapped a towel snugly around her body, and with hair dripping wet down her back, she looked at herself in the mirror again.

Shuttered eyes, firm lips, serene expression. No fire, no desire, nothing that could be used against her. Good. This was the woman she knew, this was the woman she had to be.

Still wrapped in a towel, she went to the living room to retrieve her clothes and then noted a garment bag from her closet resting on the back of a chair.

Clothes had been sent to her here. Was she supposed to wait here for Zayed then?

The idea of sitting around his suite and waiting brought back the vulnerable feeling with a vengeance. Rou went through the garment bag and grabbed a pink-and-white cotton dress with a wide, white belt and smocked neckline. She didn't like pink, but it'd cover her while she made the trip back to her wing.

It was late when Zayed came looking for her. She barely glanced up as he descended the steps into the living room, too engrossed with answering her e-mail.

"You're angry," he said, walking toward her.

She kept her eyes glued to the screen. "Not angry, just busy. I've neglected my clients while I've been here."

"I heard you refused dinner."

"I wasn't hungry."

"I can't believe that."

She finally looked up at him. "Maybe I didn't feel like another meal on a tray."

"Feeling neglected, my love?"

"Not neglected, just trapped."

With his stealthy grace, he sat down on the couch next to her. Rou wasn't having any of it. She scooted as far away as she could, but even then she could see his legs, those sinewy thighs, from beneath her lashes, and she flashed back to this afternoon when she'd sat astride those muscular thighs, and how it'd felt, skin on skin, their bodies joined.

The erotic memories flooded back, and she reached for her computer and set it between them. There would not be a repeat of this afternoon.

"Is the computer supposed to intimidate me?"

She glared at him. "Maybe I should throw it at your head instead."

He gave her a long, considering look. "You don't seem like the sort to throw things."

"I don't think you know me."

"I think I do."

She didn't want to do this, she really didn't. It was late, and she was hungry and she was hurt and angry, too. This afternoon might have meant nothing to him, but it'd been earth-shattering for her.

"Are you going to make this a guessing game, or are you going to tell me why you're angry?" he asked, picking up her computer, closing it and setting it on the table out of her reach.

"You just left me."

"You were sleeping."

"You just left."

"I had the coronation."

She folded her arms across her chest. "You couldn't wake me to say goodbye, or even leave a note?"

"I was coming back."

"You were gone for over seven hours."

"I had the coronation."

"I know!" She grabbed a pillow and squished it between her hands. "I *know*. You're set. You've got it made. Wedded, marriage consummated, and now king. A big day for you."

His expression shifted subtly, gold gaze shuttering, jaw hardening. "Yes, it's been a big day, and a long day. Is all this drama necessary? It's something my mother would do."

Drama.

Something his mother would do. The mother he'd had nothing to do with for years.

She closed her eyes, turned her face away, as stunned as if he'd thrown a punch. The words hurt as much as a physical blow, and it took her a moment to catch her breath and then another moment to get her emotions under control. "I apologize for the drama," she said when she was sure her voice was even. She even forced herself to look at him. "As you say, it's been a long day."

174 DUTY, DESIRE AND THE DESERT KING

"Let's just get some sleep. Tomorrow's a new day."

She forced a smile. "You're right."

He stood, held out a hand to her. "Come."

She looked at his hand and then up into his face. "I think I'd like to sleep here, in my own room."

His black lashes dropped, concealing the gold of his eyes. "Alone."

"Yes." She swallowed hard. "If you please."

He took a step away, made a rough sound. "If I please," he repeated, his tone strange, almost mocking. "If I please." He looked down at her, brow furrowed, lines etched at his mouth and eyes. "It's our wedding night, Rou."

A lump filled her throat and her eyes scratched and burned. She prayed that she could keep the tears from forming. "I know."

"Then what? Are we not to be together? Are we already going to live apart?"

"But we're not together. We've never been together. We've had sex, but we have no relationship. I don't even know why you'd want me to sleep in your room. What am I to you, Zayed?"

His shoulders shifted. "My wife."

"In name only," she answered, her voice barely audible.

"But it's not name only. I have vowed to protect you, I have vowed to honor you. I have vowed to put you before all women for the rest of my life. What more could I give you than that?"

Love, she wanted to say.

Friendship.

Respect.

But she couldn't say any of it, feeling horrifyingly like her mother when her parents used to fight. Her emotionally fragile mother with all those needs her father had ridiculed. Needy, clingy, pathetic, weak.

Weak.

Rou blinked, trying to clear the gritty sensation in her eyes, but it wouldn't go away.

She wasn't weak, and emotions weren't bad, and she had to find a way to reach him, had to find the words she could use, words he'd understand, words he'd relate to because so far she was just alienating him more.

Think, think. But her chest burned and her head ached and everything swirled inside her wild and chaotic. It was impossible to think clearly when she felt like this. If only he'd give her time. If only he'd sit back down, she'd try hard to calm down. If only he'd realize that this wasn't just hysterics but genuine fear. She'd never allowed anyone close to her, was never open, never struggled to communicate emotion.

But she could see he didn't understand. She could see his anger and disgust, and how he was drawing away.

Rou lifted a hand, reaching toward him, willing him to come back and take her hand or at least return so they could calm down and make themselves understood.

Zayed looked at her face and then her hand and slowly shook his head. "I wanted a strong woman, a confident woman for a reason, Rou. I don't do drama.

I don't do scenes. I can't." He headed for the stairs, taking them two at a time.

Panic and despair crashed through her. *Ask him to stay. Ask him. Ask him!*

Beg him.

Beg like Mother used to do. Beg. Sometimes it worked. Sometimes Dad stopped walking out the door when she fell to her knees and begged.

But Rou couldn't beg, and couldn't speak, and Zayed paused at the top of the stairs to look down at her. "Maybe we'll try again tomorrow," he said, perfectly cold, perfectly controlled, perfectly played, as if he were her actor father, Oscar winner Max Tornell.

She nodded, tears blinding her eyes.

"Good night, Rou."

And then he was gone, and she grabbed the pillow closest to her and, hugging it against her chest, she cried great soundless tears, her body wrenched with sobs.

This is exactly what she didn't want, exactly the scenario she feared. Men walking away. Women crying. Men long-suffering. Women breaking.

Oh God, to have him just leave like that. To have him go as though nothing mattered.

It was her father and mother all over again.

This is how it'd always played out with them. The fights. The tears. The walking out.

Rou cried as if her heart was breaking, and maybe it was, because she just understood that she was no better than her parents, and if she weren't careful she'd end up with nothing, just as they had.

CHAPTER TEN

SHE waited all morning for Zayed and he didn't come or send for her, and the more time that passed, the harder it became to wait. She wasn't good at turmoil, didn't like tension, hated that sick, nervous feeling in her stomach.

After a sleepless night she knew that she'd behaved badly. Yes, he'd left her alone for seven hours. Yes, he'd left her without saying goodbye or leaving a note, but in his defense, he did have a great many things on his mind, and daunting new responsibilities. She, of all people, should be more understanding. She, of all people, should know how stressful his life was at the moment.

Rou just wanted to apologize. She wanted to go back to the moment yesterday when she'd opened her heart to him and try again. He wasn't a bad man, he wasn't dishonest. He'd never promised her anything he didn't feel able to give.

Another hour passed and it was early afternoon now, lunch having come and gone without a word. But then just as she resolved to go to him, he appeared in her living room in his now-familiar white robe. He looked as tired as she felt.

"Hello," she said, rising from her desk, where she'd been answering e-mail, e-mail that had included responses from all of the women she'd contacted on Zayed's behalf. Three of the four women she'd e-mailed were interested in meeting him, and two were quite anxious to set up the first meet. How ironic.

"Am I interrupting?" he asked, gesturing to her computer.

"No. I'm just wrapping up." She smiled, ignoring the flutter of nerves inside her. "How is your day going?"

"It's been busy. I've been closeted with my new cabinet all morning, and then I've spent the last hour with Jesslyn and Khalid discussing Sharif's funeral."

No wonder he looked strained.

"I'm sorry about last night," she said. "I was wrong." She colored, feeling the shame of last night return. "I was selfish and thoughtless—"

"You were a new bride and you were left alone for hours on your wedding day. That couldn't have felt good."

She recognized he was trying to meet her halfway, and relief rushed through her, relief so sweet that she exhaled, letting the tension leave her tight shoulders. "I was more upset about missing the coronation. I really wanted to be there. I know it's a male-only event, but still, I care about you and I wanted to be part of it somehow."

His forehead creased. "I hadn't realized the ceremony would be followed by a formal dinner. I should have. I was there for Sharif's coronation. The dinner went on for hours." He exhaled and shook his head. "I should have at least sent word to you. I'm sorry."

"It's okay," she answered, finding that she could breathe properly for the first time since she woke up in Zayed's bed yesterday. "All this is new to both of us, and you must be as overwhelmed as I am."

"But this is my home, and my family, and my customs. I forget how little you know of our ways. However, I'd like to make it up to you. Let's go out to dinner tonight. There's a small, discreet place here in the capital city that I like very much, and it would get us out of the palace for the evening, something I think we could both use."

Rou realized she was smiling. "Yes, please. I'm curious to see what's outside these palace walls, too."

"I can meet you here at seven."

"Okay. I'll be ready."

Rou was dressed and ready by six-thirty. Manar had helped her choose the long pink-and-orange Michael Kors gown, the delicate silk fabric painted with dashes of gold and crusted with bright jewels at the plunging neckline, and then found long, gold, chandelier-style earrings for her to wear. Manar insisted Rou leave her blond hair loose but went over the ends with a flat iron to make her hair shiny, polished and smooth.

Zayed's smile was worth the effort, Rou thought, catching sight of his face as he arrived in the living room at seven sharp in a black suit, white shirt and elegant dark tie.

"You're simply stunning," he said.

She blushed and plucked at the pink-and-orange skirt. "I guess I do like some pink things."

"Well, it suits you." He smiled at her and held out his arm. "Shall we?"

"Yes, please."

Out front, their driver waited next to a black Mercedes sedan with tinted windows. Rou had a feeling as she got in the back and scooted across the seat that this was one of those armored cars with bulletproof glass. The Fehr family only traveled in the safest of vehicles.

The soft, supple leather seat gave slightly as Zayed climbed in and sat next to her. Rou's pulse quickened at Zayed's nearness. He was so close that their thighs were almost touching, and Rou pressed her knees tightly together to keep from bumping him. Was it really only a few days since their last car journey together? How much had changed between them since then!

As the driver started the car and pulled away from the palace, Zayed shot her a swift knowing glance which sent heat surging to her cheeks. "Uncomfortable?" he drawled.

She took a quick glance out the window at the palm trees lining the palace drive and shook her head. "No, just excited. I've been here a few days now, and I still

know so little about your country. You'll have to give
me a brief overview so people don't think you've
married a terribly ignorant woman."

His lips curved. "You're far from ignorant, and I
suppose I thought Sharif had told you about our
country."

"No." Her shoulders shifted. "He never talked
about himself. In fact, I didn't even know who he was
for years. It wasn't until I read a story in *Hello!*
magazine about his coronation that I realized he was
a prince."

"And yet you called him a mentor."

"He was so good to me. He was like a big brother,
or a fairy godfather. The only thing he ever asked of
me was to give back to others however I could."

"So you have, by marrying me."

She felt a tightness in her chest. "I haven't been al-
truistic, though, have I? I exacted a price."

"Every royal bride has a price. And compared to
some Fehr brides, you were quite reasonable."

"Are you serious?"

"Sharif's first wife, Zulima, was a twenty-million-
dollar bride. My father wasn't thrilled, but my mother
insisted Zulima was the right woman for Sharif."

She studied Zayed's profile in the increasingly dim
light, as dusk was just now falling and the streetlamps
hadn't yet come on. "Was she?"

"No. Sharif was already in love with Jesslyn, but
my mother wouldn't have it. She went to Jesslyn
behind Sharif's back and sent her packing. Six months

later, Sharif was engaged to Zulima, and despite their three daughters, it wasn't a happy marriage. Sharif loved Jesslyn. He'd always loved her, and even though he treated Zulima well, and loved her to the best of his ability, it wasn't enough for Zulima and she never forgave Sharif for loving Jesslyn first."

"But they, Jesslyn and Sharif, found each other again."

His gaze was fixed on the city street with its modern office buildings, throng of taxis and crowded sidewalks. "It wasn't long enough," he said after a moment. "Not after nine years apart. They should have had more time."

The lump was back in her throat. "It's probably small comfort for you, but at least their love will carry on. They made Prince Tahir and he's an incredible little boy. Smart, beautiful, mischievous. He'll be a great comfort to Jesslyn as he grows older."

"To all of us," Zayed added, turning to look at her, his expression grim. "In my ceremony last night I vowed to protect my nephew and my country until Tahir is old enough to take the throne. I was honored to have so many of our friends and neighbors there pledging their support, and vowing to guard my nephew as their own—King Malik Nuri of Baraka, his brother Kalen Nuri, Sultan of Ouaha, Sheikh Tair, the great desert chieftain." Zayed's voice roughened. "They have all promised to protect Sarq and young Tahir until he is of age to rule. Their loyalty is a testament to their feelings for my late brother."

She reached out, covered his hand with hers. "He was very loved, and he would be very grateful that you have come home to serve in his place."

He lifted her hand to his mouth, kissed the back. "Thank you, *laeela*. But this is supposed to be a celebration of our marriage, and yet all I do is talk about my family."

"But I want to know about your family. I want to know as much as I can."

He forced a smile, but it failed to reach his eyes. "Then let me tell you about Sarq and Isi, the capital city."

For the next few minutes he told her that Sarq, a small country that bordered part of the Arabian Sea, was ninety percent Muslim, and yet it was a very tolerant country, very open and receptive to all people and all cultures. Because of its proximity to the Arabian Sea, Sarq was enjoying its new reputation as a year-round resort destination.

"After a fifteen-year building boom, we now have more luxury beach resorts than any other Middle Eastern country outside of Dubai and the U.A.E." Zayed's eyes narrowed as they paused at the corner for a red light and a trio of girls in veils dashed across the street giggling. "I was part of that building boom. I'm probably the largest investor in the five biggest luxury resorts, but I'm beginning to think it was a mistake. My father was the one who first opened the door to development, and Sharif inherited my father's liberal policies, but I think he should have limited the growth more than he did."

"It must have been hard for Sharif to say no to you."

"I certainly didn't make it easy, and Khalid and I had quite a few rows about what I was doing to the environment. I thought Khalid was ridiculous—protecting sand dunes when we could turn Sarq into a thriving and competitive world economy—but now I think he's right. The vanishing sand dunes represent vanishing wildlife and I hate to think of my children growing up in a country without nature, or the animals and plants I knew as a boy."

They were passing through a quieter neighborhood now, away from the bustle of hotels and the business district. The buildings were older here and typical of historic Islamic architecture with whitewashed facades marked by arches, turrets and columns.

Moments later, the limousine drew to a stop outside a residential-looking building. Rou peered out the window at the semidark street. Expensive homes lined the street. She saw no sign of a restaurant or public facility. "I thought we were going out for dinner."

"We are. You'll see."

Outside, on the pavement, they climbed three steps to an elegant front door. The door looked like any door in a residential area, but when the sheikh rang the doorbell, it opened silently and they entered into a square hall painted the darkest chocolate, the only light that of an enormous chandelier.

A dark-suited man appeared, bowed. "King Fehr, welcome. I have a table waiting."

"Where are we?" she whispered as Zayed took her elbow.

"It's a private club, very exclusive."

"Very exclusive if no one knows it's here."

"Membership is steep," he conceded, "but people are happy to pay it if they can be assured of privacy. Security. Peace of mind." The edge of his mouth lifted. "For many in my circle, peace of mind is a precious commodity and worth every penny."

She shot him a knowing glance. "You own the club, don't you? And twenty more like it around the world."

He wasn't quite able to hide his surprise. "How do you know?"

"I went online this morning and read your company's profile and researched your investment portfolio." She saw the look he gave her, and she added, "I thought I should know as much as I could about my husband."

"Smart woman," he said with a soft laugh.

They passed through a room with low couches covered in leopard print. Candles flickered on equally low square tables, and the room smelled fresh, crisp, like green apples crossed with freshly mown grass, and it was a tantalizing scent.

Six to eight white lacquered tables were scattered around the dining room, while the walls were upholstered in rich brown suede. Silver chargers and candles gleamed on all the tables, even the empty ones.

"We practically have the place to ourselves," Rou noted as she sat down at their corner table.

"A luxury I'm very grateful for tonight," he answered, and for the first time Rou saw traces of fatigue in his face. Lines at his eyes, shadows beneath his eyes.

"This is a huge change for you, isn't it?"

"It's a job I certainly never wanted, not even as a boy. Father made it clear that the job was an all-consuming one, as well as weighted with enormous responsibilities, and yet Sharif never complained, nor made us younger brothers feel guilty that he was the one with so much pressure on his shoulders."

She studied his face in the restaurant's candlelight. The new fine lines and shadows she was seeing there only heightened his appeal. He looked older, stronger, more mature. "You will miss your old life, I think."

His lips twisted. "I loved living in Monte Carlo and having apartments in London and New York. I enjoyed business and travel. But I think what I loved best was that my family seemed safe. I realize now it was an illusion—anything bad can happen at any time—but I was under the impression that as long as I stayed away, they were protected." His bitter smile faded. "I will miss that secure thought more than Monte Carlo or my freedom. I know now none of us will ever be safe."

"Life is never safe," she said softly. "But just because it's not safe, doesn't mean it's cursed."

"No, I am cursed. I know the moment it happened. Even my family will tell you."

She pushed her empty water glass away from her. "Jesslyn did say something," she admitted.

"When?"

"The morning of our wedding. She came to my room with a gift, and as she was leaving she told me not to listen to the gossip about you...about the curse." Rou looked at him, unable to hide her worry. "I understand from the little she said that something happened in your past. She didn't go into details and I didn't ask, but I'd like to know what this dark cloud is that hangs above you."

"It's more than a dark cloud. The curse has struck again. It killed Sharif."

"Jesslyn said Sharif didn't believe in the curse."

He made a rough sound. "Fine. He didn't believe in the curse, but where is he today?"

Her eyes met his and held. "Tell me what happened. Please."

"It's a terrible story, especially for a romantic night out."

"But we have time, and no one will interrupt us."

His gaze searched hers. "It might change how you feel about me."

She made a face. "Maybe for the better."

He grimaced. "Was that a joke, Dr. Tornell?"

"A bad one."

"Well, I liked it. A little humor can go a long way when things are difficult." He reached out, took her hand in his and held it for a moment before letting it go. "You really want to know?"

"Yes."

"Then I'll give you the short version. It's all I think

I can manage tonight." He paused, stared off across the restaurant, already lost in thought.

After a moment he opened his mouth to speak, but closed it without uttering a word. Zayed shook his head slowly, rubbed his brow, and then his lip and then looked at Rou. "I fell in love with a neighbor's wife. I was seventeen. She was twenty-four. She was very beautiful. Very, very beautiful. And very elegant and kind and charming. When she laughed I thought it was the most wonderful sound in the world."

He stopped, looked down at the table where his hand was splayed, fingers pressed to the surface. "Nur was from Dubai, a princess, and her marriage to this neighboring sheikh was arranged. Her husband wasn't a close friend of my father's, but an acquaintance, and we would see them several times a year. I never spent time alone with her, just bumping into her at the horse races, at parties, formal dinners, things like that."

Rou watched his face as he talked, watched the emotion and agony flicker across, one after the other. She couldn't have interrupted him now even if she wanted to.

"Being seventeen, I had to let her know how I felt. I loved her. I loved her as much as I have ever loved anyone. I knew she was married. But I wanted her for myself."

He looked up, into Rou's eyes. "We never slept together. I never even kissed her. There was no physical contact, nothing other than my professed love…" His voice faded, and he sat, jaw clenched, skin pulled taut over hard cheekbones. "And then she disappeared. Gone. For a couple weeks no one knew what had happened. And then word came that she was dead. Her husband, suspecting her of infidelity, had her killed."

Zayed's jaw worked, eyes narrowed in tangible pain. "I would have given my life for her. I wanted nothing more than to love her. And my love, my stupidity, my impulsiveness and arrogance killed her. He had her stoned all because I lacked self-control."

Rou sat, hands pressed to her chest. She couldn't speak. Couldn't. She'd dealt with guilt and tragedies as part of her practice, but this, this was the kind of guilt that crushed a man.

"She was innocent," he added quietly. "She viewed me as a younger brother. She treated me kindly, and yes, she'd smile her dazzling smiles at me, but it was because I amused her. And I still sometimes think of her, and her final day…her final hours. I imagine her terror. I can almost feel her pain."

"But if you didn't ever touch her…if you never slept with her…?" Rou whispered her questions.

"It was a matter of shame. *Hshuma,*" he said, using the Arabic word, his long black eyelashes dropping, brushing the sweep of his high, hard cheekbones. "It's a concept you don't have in the West, not the way we do. While you may have guilt, we have *hshuma*, and it means that others know you've done wrong, and that is for us the worst sin of all. One must make atonement, set things right, and the way you do that is to destroy what has brought shame on you. If your eye has sinned, you pluck out the eye. If the hand has sinned, you cut off the hand."

"And if the wife has sinned?"

He smiled a ghostly smile, while the gold eyes revealed hatred and horror. "You put her to death."

She knew he was being sarcastic, but still, his words sent a shudder down her spine.

"Her husband and his family feel they acted properly," he continued after a moment. "But I paid no price. So we were cursed."

"But you did pay a price," she said softly after a moment. "You lost the person you loved most. No price could be greater than that."

"There are many who believe it wasn't enough. Our neighbor, the sheikh, demanded my father hold me accountable. My father refused to condemn me to death. Instead he sent me away to England to finish school. People believe that my father's refusal to hold me accountable cursed us. Thus the deaths of my sisters, my father, and now Sharif."

It made sense in a terribly nightmarish, stomach-churning sort of way. It also finally explained why Zayed avoided close ties and ended relationships when they turned serious. And little wonder he asked her to find him a bride when it became apparent he needed to marry. He wasn't marrying for love, he wasn't offering his heart, he couldn't. He was still in love with Nur.

"I'm so sorry," she said, thinking the words sounded pathetic at best. "I'm sorry for all of you—"

"Don't be sorry for me," he interrupted, eyes blazing. "I deserve every wretched punishment, but my family, especially my sisters, my brother…they were innocent, just like Nur."

"What if it's not a curse? What if it's just really lousy luck?"

"Another Western word for fate or karma."

"Yes, there's cause and effect, everything has cause and effect, but no one in your family believes that you have anything to do with the family's losses."

"But I believe, and that is enough."

In that moment, all the pieces came together for Rou. She saw him clearly, the outline and shape as well as the smaller pieces that made the man.

He wasn't cold and arrogant, wasn't selfish. He wasn't spoiled and egotistical. He was a man who was alone and lonely, a man tormented by a past, a man so afraid of hurting those he loved that he'd closed himself off from everyone.

This is why she'd been so afraid of him. He was hurt just like her.

It broke another bit of her heart, damaging that armor she'd once kept so tightly around herself. What armor could protect her against him?

Her chest tightened, ached, and she realized that little by little she was falling for him. A man who would never love her back.

As the waiter approached, Rou told herself that she

didn't need his love. She told herself that a partnership would be enough. Maybe romantic love wasn't as important in this case, not if they respected and supported each other.

Maybe respect and shared goals would be enough.

There was a very good chance it'd have to be enough.

Suppressing her doubts, suppressing her emotions, suppressing all her needs, she reached for his hand. Zayed needed a wife. She would find a way to be that wife.

"Let's eat and leave," she said softly. "Let's just go back to the palace and be quiet and not think. Not think about curses or losses, not tonight. There'll be plenty of time for that tomorrow."

CHAPTER ELEVEN

ON RETURNING to the palace they retreated to Zayed's wing, where his rooms were dimly lit by the soft glow of candles and smelled faintly of fragrant sandalwood.

"It's nice," Rou said, taking in the way the candlelight flickered, casting long, dancing shadows on the walls and stone floor.

"I think my valet is determined to help me in the romance department," Zayed said wryly. "He was worried when we didn't spend last night together."

She set her small gold bag on the table behind his blue velvet couch. "He said that?"

"No, but he asked enough indirect questions to make me understand that he was concerned and ready and willing to help, should I only seek his advice."

Her lips curved. "I take it you did not ask for any."

"I did not," he affirmed, approaching her.

Rou's pulse jumped as he neared. When they were sitting down with a table between them he was so much less imposing, but standing, he was tall and muscular, handsome and elegant, and the combination of all those factors made him far too intimidating.

He reached for her, putting an arm around her waist, and then drawing her toward him. The flutter in her middle became a wild thudding. The whole body contact thing was still alarming. As was the relationship itself. She still couldn't quite believe they were together…married…and she didn't quite know how to reconcile herself to the concept of *married* life.

His head lowered, his lips brushed her ear. "I can see the wheels turning, Dr. Tornell. You live in a state of constant analysis."

His body was hard and yet warm, and that warmth penetrated her dress and skin, sinking all the way into her bones. It was such a seductive heat, promising all kinds of ease and pleasure. "I like to use my brain."

"It's an excellent brain, but your body is excellent, too."

Her heart hammered. "Maybe we should spend a little more time getting to know each other before we start getting to know each other's bodies."

He kissed the side of her neck. "We can't do both at the same time?"

How could just one kiss on her neck make her so weak? It wasn't fair that he seemed to know where every nerve ending lay, too. Rou closed her eyes, trying to block the delicious sensations coursing through her so she could focus on what was important—and that was their relationship. "It's not quite as effective. The body is easier to gratify."

He tilted her head back, kissed beneath her jaw. "I

don't know about that. You're quite a challenge, my dear doctor."

If only he knew the truth, she thought, her breath catching as his lips moved along her sensitive jaw, and the curl of desire turned into something hotter, sharper, more urgent.

He'd always been gorgeous, but these past few days he was more than just a physically attractive man. He appealed to something deeper in her, appealed to a part of her that no one else could touch. It was bittersweet to know that he had such power over her, too.

What if she fell for him the way Angela did? What if she fell hard?

Her breath came shallowly as he kissed the corner of her mouth and his hands slid up her back, shaping her to him.

He was making her remember needs and emotions, making her want those needs and emotions, and yet he'd never once promised anything other than respect and protection. But they would be cold bedfellows.

Be careful, a little voice inside her head warned her. *You're so close to disaster here. So close to total destruction.*

Rou's self-preservation struck back, chasing away the fog of desire. She couldn't afford to give him all the power. She had to remain an equal, a true partner. It was the only way for their relationship to survive. She pushed back from him now, creating space so that she could think properly.

"It's late," she said, hoping her voice was even, hoping he wouldn't know how difficult it was to break away from him. "I should return to my room."

"But these are our rooms now. Everything has been brought here from your suite, and that wing of the palace has been closed again."

She took another step back in her high, slim heels, her hands going to her hips. "Is that why you took me out for dinner? So the staff could scurry around and move me into your rooms without me protesting?"

"*Laeela*, we are married, it's proper that we share rooms."

"Your valet's peace of mind is more important than mine?"

Zayed laughed, a low, husky, sexy laugh that sent a ripple of awareness through her. He was so very male, and so very primal, and so very comfortable. Too comfortable.

"I'm not trying to be funny, Zayed," she added, feeling ridiculously emotional, which meant she was tired. She only became emotional when she needed sleep, and after two sleepless nights, sleep was what she craved most right now and there was no way she could get the sleep she needed in Zayed's bed. "I haven't slept well in days."

Zayed, with that uncanny ability of his to read her mind, smiled down at her. "You will be able to sleep here in our room just fine. I won't bite you, and I promise not to pounce on you."

She never understood how he always knew what she was thinking. "It's just that I'm used to sleeping alone. I've never spent the night with a man."

He gold gaze warmed. "It's not much different from napping with me, except the night is longer."

"But I'll feel you in the bed. I'll know you're there."

"Can't that be a good thing?"

A disturbing thing, she answered silently, aware that he still held her in the crook of his arm, aware that her pulse was now pounding like mad. Looking up into his face she felt an inexplicable tightness in her chest, which made catching her breath a struggle.

How was it possible that this man, this gorgeous man, this *king,* was her husband?

"Shall we go to bed?" he asked, his voice deepening.

"Only if we can build a wall of pillows between us," she answered coolly.

"What are you afraid of? I've promised you I won't seduce you tonight. You'll sleep unmolested, *laeela.*"

What was she afraid of? *I'm afraid of you,* she wanted to tell him. *Afraid that I've fallen in love with a man who will never love me back.* But she held back the words, keeping the truth to herself as she understood the importance of appearances and the need for dignity.

With her emotions now well under control, she managed a mocking smile. "Just afraid of not getting the rest I need. But know that if you do get amorous I will poke you, and it'll hurt."

And Zayed, he of the ghosts and dark, haunted past,

laughed, a rich, boyish laugh, which made his lips curve and his eyes light up. "You know, you are the first woman who has threatened me if I touched her."

"Because I'm the first woman you've tried to seduce that has any common sense."

Rou saw his eyes warm, the golden depths gleaming, and she realized belatedly that he loved the challenge she presented him. It stirred him, brought out the primal male in him. Not something she wanted before she slipped between his sheets. "I hope Manar remembered to pack my nightgown," she said.

"I would hope not," he answered. "You'll sleep better naked—"

"Ha!"

"But if she didn't," he continued with a grin, "I'm sure I can find a shirt for you to sleep in. But there is your closet. Have a look, see what you can find."

Rou opened the doors to the closet and was greeted by a rainbow of color and a low dresser filled with her silk and satin underwear, which did include a nightgown or two. She grabbed the first gown she found, a sleek ivory number made of silk with the thinnest of shoulder straps, and after changing in the ensuite bathroom, Rou cleaned her teeth and combed her hair, giving the blond strands a vigorous brushing before heading for Zayed's oversize bed.

Leaving the bathroom, she walked toward the bed as though she didn't have a care in the world, walked as if it were a Sunday stroll in the park, walked as if oblivious to the fact that Zayed sat in an armchair watching her, a smile playing at his sensual mouth.

Beast, she muttered to herself. *He's no gentleman,* she added, as she reached the bed and realized she didn't know which side he preferred to sleep on.

Rou hesitated, and, gritting her teeth, turned toward Zayed, aware that she was giving him an eyeful of silk-clad curves. The nightgown was ridiculously form-fitting and far more sheer than a nightgown needed to be. "Which side do you sleep on?"

His gaze traveled slowly, appreciatively, from her head to her bare feet and then back up again, lingering indecently long at the juncture of her thighs and then her breasts. "I usually just sleep in the middle."

She could feel her nipples harden beneath his gaze, and it took all of her self-control not to cover herself. "Unfortunately tonight you only get *half* the bed. Which *half* is it to be?"

"The half you're sleeping on."

Heat stormed her cheeks, burning her skin. "You promised me."

"But that was before you came out looking like whipped cream, vanilla ice cream and marshmallow sauce." He rested his gaze on her face, and she saw the hunger in his eyes. He wasn't even trying to hide it. "I could very easily eat you right now," he added.

From the look on his face she didn't doubt it. "Well, I'm sleeping here, on this side, and you'll just have to take the other side, and tomorrow we can discuss whatever else we need to discuss." Then, climbing into the bed, she plumped a pillow beneath her head, pulled the covers up to her neck and closed her eyes. "Good night."

"Good night."

Zayed didn't immediately join her in bed. He'd said earlier at the club he had reading to do, and although she hadn't thought she could sleep in his room, in his bed, he dimmed all the lights except for his reading lamp and then settled in to read for hours.

Rou gave up trying to stay awake, and the next time she woke, she did because she was very warm. Very, very warm, and a little too confined.

Frowning, she tugged on the covers, trying to free herself and then realized it wasn't the covers pinning her down. It was the big male arm attached to the big male body holding her snugly around her middle and securely against his body.

She stiffened in alarm. Yes, they'd slept close yesterday after they'd made love, but that was different. They'd had sex and there was the whole postcoital cuddle thing, but she didn't just cuddle on demand. And she didn't cuddle when she was sleeping. Sleep was sleep.

"Take a deep breath in, now exhale," Zayed said, his voice raspy with sleep. "Do it again—"

"Maybe I'll relax if you move over."

"Maybe you need to address your intimacy issues."

She lifted her head, looked over her shoulder at him. "My intimacy issues? Mine?"

He laughed softly, his breath warm against the back of her neck. "Calm down before you get all excited.

You'll never fall back asleep if you're kicking and screaming."

She held herself as rigid as she could. "I'm not kicking or screaming. I'm just communicating my discomfort at being held so close."

"But it feels good."

"To you."

"And you."

She threw an elbow, jabbing him in the ribs. "It doesn't feel good to me. You don't feel good to me. And trying to convince me that it does is a waste of time and breath."

"Really?"

All of a sudden she realized that he wasn't merely holding her around the waist anymore. His arm was higher on her rib cage, and his hand was dangerously close to her breast. "Zayed."

"Yes, love?"

She closed her eyes, held her breath, tried to ignore the deliciously pleasurable sensation of his fingers stroking the soft skin beneath her breast and then the soft fullness of the side. He had the seductive touch of the devil, she thought, lips parting in silent protest as his palm circled over her jutting nipple, making her entire breast tighten and ache. "I'm not your love," she gasped defiantly.

"No, you're my wife," he answered, flipping her onto her back and settling between her legs. He supported his weight on his arm but dipped his head to kiss her, his mouth covering hers in a hard, urgent kiss that demanded a response. Rou's heart pounded hard and her veins felt thick with hot desire.

So many things in life didn't feel right, but this did, she thought, twining her arms around his neck to hold him close as he parted her lips and drew fire with the tip of his tongue against her own.

His tongue played her lips and tongue, wakening nerves and heightening sensitivity until her hips were arching helplessly against his, her body craving release. But Zayed wasn't in the mood to rush, and he sucked on her tongue, a fierce rhythmic caress that made Rou wriggle and pant, more desperate than ever for relief.

"Yes, *laeela*?" he murmured against her mouth, stroking her hair back from her flushed face.

"You know what I want."

"I'm afraid I don't." He nipped her neck with his teeth. "Apparently it doesn't feel good when I touch you."

She nearly groaned with frustration as he flicked the tip of his tongue over the pulse running below her ear. It was a move designed to make her toes curl and her spine arch and her belly ache and it was regrettably most successful. "It feels good," she choked from between gritted teeth.

"What was that?"

He was touching her, caressing her, licking her, and there was no way to think clearly, rationally, when he made her body feel like a lovely sweet. "I was wrong," she gritted. "You do feel good." And then she gasped as his lips found her nipple through the cool silk of her nightgown. His mouth was so hot against her skin, and her breasts, already swollen, grew even more heavy and sensitive as he sucked on the nipple, making the fabric wet, which felt almost cold against her feverish skin.

She was beyond control now, and, wrapping her arms around his shoulders, she ground her hips up against him. He groaned against her breast as she discovered the rigid length of his erection straining against his thin cotton pajama pants. Wantonly she pressed and rubbed herself against him, feeling the hard shaft, the thick smooth head, the satisfying length.

He groaned again as her movements grew wilder, more desperate, her legs kicking up her nightgown to tangle with his. And then his control snapped, and he shoved the delicate fabric up over her hips, exposing her legs and the blond curls at the juncture of her thighs. Head lifted, he watched her as he stroked a hand over her flat belly and hip and then back up again to the other side.

"You're so damn beautiful," he said, voice husky. "You make resisting you very difficult."

She'd been biting her lip as his fingertips caressed her stomach and hip bones, the sensitive inner thigh and outer thigh and then just when she didn't think she could stand it, he'd found the cleft of her, her body hot and liquid and melting for him. "Then don't," she panted. "Because I don't think I can handle resistance now."

He parted her knees with his own, pushing her legs

wide enough to accommodate his body and then he was between her thighs, the silken knob of his erection pressing against her body. With a smooth, hard thrust he entered her, and she inhaled sharply as he filled her, pleasuring her.

Amazing, she thought, pressing her mouth to his shoulder, amazing as he drove into her again and again, waking every nerve with each hot, hard, insistent thrust until she gave up control, giving her body and will over to him. The orgasm was wrenching, catching her by surprise and sending shock waves of sensation through her as her body tightened and spasmed around his. And just when she thought it was over, she was hit by another ripple of pleasure, and the tension started to build all over again, wave after wave building even hotter, higher into a second orgasm even more powerful and unrelenting than the first.

Rou went limp beneath Zayed, perspiration beading her skin, her pulse still racing. She opened an eye and looked at him. He was trying hard not to laugh. "Are you alive?" he asked.

"Barely."

"Two, *laeela*? Isn't that a bit greedy of you?"

She blushed and wrinkled her nose, hating that she even had to ask him about his own satisfaction. "Did you...uh, um...come?"

His lips twitched and his warm eyes glowed. "Yes, I managed, thank you."

"It's not my fault," she protested defensively.

"You're the one that does this to me. You weren't content to stop at one—"

"I wondered if you could manage two."

"And thanks to you, I did."

He lowered his head, kissed her gently, and again. "My iceberg runs hot," he murmured against her mouth before kissing her again.

And Rou's heart just turned over. She loved him.

She loved him.

She was in such trouble now because she loved him, and her gorgeous, brilliant, sexy, tormented husband loved another.

There were no words. She had no words, so she met his kiss with hunger and urgency, using her lips to convey what her heart longed to say.

She loved him. And she hoped, prayed, that maybe one day he'd love her back. Even just a little bit.

The next morning, Zayed had breakfast brought to Rou in bed. Rou had still been sleeping when Manar arrived with a tray filled with fruits and pastries, yogurt, juice and coffee. Zayed waited while Manar arranged the tray on Rou's lap. "I've a phone conference in a few minutes," he told Rou, "but once I'm done I'll return for you and then we're going to sneak away."

She was adding cream to her coffee and nearly spilled the cream when she jerked her head up to look at him. He'd showered already and dressed and looked immaculate with his combed hair, smooth jaw and pristine robes. "Sneak where?"

"To my summer palace in Cala. It's a beautiful retreat right on the water, and we do need a honeymoon."

She flushed at the mention of honeymoon, remembering how they'd spent the very early hours of the morning. "Can you afford to leave now?"

"We can get away for a few days." He reached out, ran a hand over her tousled hair. "I'll have Manar pack you a bag, okay?"

Rou clasped her cup and nodded, smiling. "Yes. Yes, please."

Two hours later they were in his helicopter, leaving the capital city of Isi for the beach resort of Cala. Another woman might have felt dazed by the speed with which Zayed accomplished things, but Rou was accustomed to multitasking and she appreciated his efficiency, although she was still rather awed by the number of people who worked for him as well as the number of toys he owned. Apparently there were jets and yachts, helicopters and luxury automobiles, penthouses, apartments, palaces.

Sixty minutes into the flight, Zayed pointed to the deep blue water below. "The sea," he said, and then another fifteen minutes later he pointed to a sprawling white complex. "My palace."

His palace. She shot him a sidelong glance, repeating his words. She'd married a man with palaces. She'd married a man who'd become king. She'd married.

So strange. So not the way life was going to be.

As the helicopter slowly descended onto a helipad on one of the palace wings, she got a better glimpse of the palace's fanciful architecture. Turrets and towers, arched windows, extensive latticework, thick stone walls all painted a dazzling white.

Date palms and coconut palms grew along the corners of the house, tall, slim trunks in stark contrast to the white walls. Just before the helicopter set down, Rou caught a glimpse of a pool inside a walled garden that overlooked the ocean, and Rou couldn't resist reaching for Zayed's hand as excitement bubbled up inside her. This was going to be fun.

Fun.

When was the last time she had fun?

And, turning her head, she caught Zayed's eye, and she smiled at him. He lifted her hand to his mouth, kissed the inside of her wrist, giving her hope that yes, maybe one day, he would love her. Maybe it wasn't such an impossible dream.

The next four days were spent making love, sleeping in, sunning by the pool, swimming in the sea and consuming more food and drink than Rou could remember in years.

Zayed was perfectly attentive and perfectly wonderful, telling her stories, making her laugh, and making her fall even more in love with him.

Rou knew on Thursday morning he was scheduled to fly back to Isi for a meeting with his cabinet. The final plans were also being made for Sharif's funeral, and Zayed wanted to sit with Jesslyn and discuss all the details in person. It'd be a long day in the capital city, but then he'd jump into the helicopter and return that night.

Thursday morning when Zayed left the bed, Rou sat up, too. "Maybe I should go with you," she suggested. "I could help somehow."

He was heading into the enormous limestone bathroom and paused naked in the door. "It's gloomy at the palace in Isi—this place is full of sunshine. Stay. Relax. You'll have a better time."

"But what if you can't wrap up everything in a day? What if you have to stay overnight?"

He shrugged, unconcerned. "Then I'd stay overnight and return first thing in the morning. And don't you have work to do? I haven't seen you check your e-mail once since we arrived. Maybe you can use the time to get caught up on your work, too."

He was right. Her clients were probably in a panic because she had never been so out of touch or unresponsive before, but working here in Cala wasn't like working in San Francisco. San Francisco was often filled with fog and chilly mists, which made sitting at a desk, concentrating at a computer far easier than here on the sunny dry coast where olive and orange trees studded the lawn, and a huge aquamarine pool shimmered, beckoning whenever one looked out the window.

"All right. I'll work while you work. But do come back tonight if you can. It won't be the same without you."

CHAPTER TWELVE

HE DIDN'T return that night.

Or the next.

Or call, or send word to say when he'd return.

It hurt her feelings, but she wasn't going to let him upset her this time. She knew he had many responsibilities and worries, knew that his entire family was under pressure and looking to him for strength and support, which made her vow not to add to the pressure.

She'd help him by making things easier, and keeping things calm, so she focused on staying busy those first few days he was gone, knowing that the more she got done now, the more free time she'd have to spend with Zayed once he returned. And she wanted that time with him, she craved time with him, having become quite attached to him and his company already.

He was smart and funny and interesting and entertaining. When he was there with her, she couldn't imagine anyone more attentive, but when he was gone…

She sighed and shook her head as she walked along the private beach in front of the palace, gentle waves lapping at her feet. The water was cool and the damp, firm sand mushed between her toes. She loved it here, loved the sun and sea and tang of salt in the air, but she felt very alone, too.

Because when Zayed was gone, he wasn't merely absent, he was completely gone. So completely that it stirred up old memories, childhood memories of being scuttled away, shoved off, abandoned. When her father drank, he'd forget to come for her. When her mother went into a depression, she couldn't care for her. When the courts finally gave custody of her to her grandmother in England, her mother took her life.

Even though she was an adult now, even though she was successful and polished and accomplished, she didn't know if people would be there for her when she needed them, didn't trust that those she loved would be available, accessible, when she reached out to them.

But fear and doubt only beget fear and doubt, she reminded herself, leaving the creamy crescent cove for the palace gardens. Climbing the old stone stairs toward the pool level she vowed not to give in to fear or insecurity, not this time. Zayed was working, that was all. She had work to do, too, and when she tired of working, she'd find fun things to do to help the time pass more quickly.

For the rest of the morning Rou sat out by the pool in a swimsuit and worked in the shade of a giant umbrella on her computer, writing an essay for a women's magazine, and preparing a speech she was to give in Chicago in two months' time. And then, at noon, when there was no more work to do, she returned to her room, showered and changed into a turquoise-and-ivory-embroidered silk tunic, ivory capris and fun wedge sandals with turquoise stones. Dressed, she sent for the palace butler and asked if he could make arrangements with one of the palace drivers to take her into town so she could shop in the colorful, old city market bazaar.

The butler was appalled that she'd want to go someplace so loud and crowded, never mind dirty. "It's Saturday and it'll be filled with shoppers and tourists. You won't enjoy yourself. There are only little stalls selling copper and pots, died yarn and foodstuffs, nothing you'd like."

"But that's exactly what I want to see. The palace isn't Sarq, and Cala has such a fascinating history, I'd love the chance to explore."

"I should ask His Highness."

"No," she said clearly, firmly, "you do not need to ask His Highness if I can leave the palace. I am just heading into town, and I'm certain you will send a few bodyguards with me, so there's no reason for alarm."

The butler did send a complete security detail with her, which meant four bodyguards, but even their close watch couldn't upset her as they drove the three miles into town.

Rou watched the passing scenery with great interest, excited by the prospect of seeing the historic seaport and then exploring the famous bazaar. She'd brought along her wallet, hoping she might find something she could give to Zayed as a belated wedding gift. He'd given her jewels and a new wardrobe, but so far she'd given him nothing, not having had the opportunity to shop. Today she might find something with which to surprise him.

The market was as crowded as the butler had said it'd be, with hundreds of robed men and veiled women jamming between the narrow stalls to haggle over prices and make purchases for the coming week.

Rou wandered for nearly two hours, stopping once midafternoon for a cup of mint tea at a corner shop. The store owner was delighted she'd chosen his shop and sent over a plate of almond cookies along with the tea. The bodyguards circled her as she munched on the cookies and sipped the strong tea. She appreciated their zealousness but did find it hard to relax and soak up the atmosphere when all she could see were their dark jackets and the bulge of guns beneath.

Late afternoon she concluded her shopping by buying bread and cheese, chocolate and fruit, along with some bottles of a lemony, fizzy drink. She'd ask the kitchen staff to save everything for her until Zayed returned, and then she'd surprise him with a picnic on the beach.

Tired, but pleased with her afternoon, she returned to the palace only to discover that Zayed had called while she was gone. He wouldn't be back for days.

Still clutching the paper-wrapped bread and bags of fruit and cheese, Rou stared unhappily at the butler who'd just given her the news. "Did he say when he'd return?"

"No, Your Highness. He just said 'days.'"

Days. Days could be a few days, or a week. Maybe even longer.

She swallowed her disappointment, handed over her purchases and headed for her room with its view of the sea. Rou stood at the narrow arched window for long minutes, watching the waves roll toward shore and then break in white foamy crests against the sand.

Days. He wouldn't be back for days. What did that mean?

After a half hour and much frustration and endless soul-searching, Rou decided she'd speak to him herself, and as her cell phone didn't get coverage here in Cala, she'd just have to use the palace phone. Leaving her room, she went in search of the crusty old butler to ask for a house phone.

The butler said he'd place the call for her. Rou stiffened at the rebuke in his voice. "If you'll just point me to a phone, I can call."

"Do you have his number?"

"His cell, yes."

"The royal family does not use wireless phones in the palace. They only use select palace numbers. Now if you'd like me to place the call—"

"No." Rou's voice shook with emotion. "He's my husband. I want to call him. I need to be able to call him without butlers and valets and staff running interference."

The butler's expression hardened with reproach. "I am not interfering, Your Highness, merely trying to help." And then he turned and walked away, narrow back ramrod straight.

He didn't understand. She hadn't said he was interfering but what did she expect? English wasn't his first language, and she realized he wasn't accustomed to dealing with Western women, and Western women's expectations.

Rou took a breath, and then another, to calm herself. Nothing was simple here. She couldn't do the smallest of tasks without needing assistance. She hated the lack of independence, hated asking for help, but at this point she wanted to talk to Zayed more than anything, and if she needed the butler's help, she'd take his help.

Rou set off after him, and with a brief but sincere apology, she told him she was sorry and yes, she'd please like him to help her place the call to King Fehr.

The butler nodded and gestured for her to follow. Rou sat in a chair waiting while he dialed the palace in Isi and made a request with one of the Isi palace staff that they put him in touch with His Highness, King Zayed, as the king's wife was wanting to speak to him.

Several minutes passed while different palace staff relayed messages and then relayed them back to the butler in Cala. In the end, the butler hung up the phone without Rou being able to speak to Zayed.

"I'm sorry, Your Highness. The king is in meetings, but his staff has promised to leave him a message that you phoned."

She smiled brightly, but as she turned away, the disappointment tore through her, making a mockery of all her good intentions. She didn't want to be difficult, didn't want to be demanding, but she also didn't want to feel so insignificant, and worse, so very alone.

But she was alone.

And she was beginning to worry that everything she feared about marriage, everything she feared about becoming dependent and losing her individuality, losing her very sense of self, was happening.

While Zayed took care of business in Isi, she drifted around the Cala palace waiting for him to acknowledge her. Every thought these past few days had been about Zayed, for Zayed. Every breath was bated, waiting, waiting, just as she'd waited for her parents, waited for her mother to stop crying, waited for her father to stop drinking, waited for someone to come for her, someone to remember her.

This is why she'd never wanted to marry. This is why she'd been afraid to love.

This is why waiting left her feeling terrifyingly close to despair.

A full week passed before the helicopter buzzed the summer palace, and Rou went to the window, knowing it was Zayed's helicopter, knowing it meant he'd returned. After ten days' absence he'd returned.

She was glad, and yet scared and didn't know what to think, or feel. She waited in her room for an hour after the helicopter's arrival, waited for him to come see her, or at least send for her, but the minutes crawled by without a sign of him.

Disappointed, but determined to stay positive, she forced herself to stop pacing, forced herself to pick up a book and try to distract herself until Zayed did come. He would come. He hadn't seen her in ten days. He must miss her a little.

She certainly missed him. And she hadn't been really lonely until the last few days, when it hit her how isolated she'd become. Her cell phone didn't work and her e-mail was sporadic. She was beginning to miss her life, and the work she did, and the activity that had kept her from thinking too much about things she couldn't change.

And the hours kept ticking by without Zayed.

She squeezed her eyes shut when hot, salty tears stung her eyes. *You can't cry,* she told herself. *He's just busy. He doesn't realize how excited you are, or how much you want to see him. If he knew, he'd be here. If he knew, he'd come.*

But her words of comfort failed to comfort. They had a painfully familiar ring to them. And it was with a lurch she realized she'd told herself the same thing as a girl when she'd waited for her father to come see her on his appointed days. She'd wait in her mother's hallway in a little chair, her doll in her arms, her coat buttoned up. She'd wait and wait and tell herself her handsome, dashing father was on his way. He hadn't forgotten her. He was just busy….

Rou covered her face with her hands and began to

cry, silent, agonizing tears that were torn from the deepest, darkest corner of her heart.

She, who'd never wanted to marry, had married a man just like her absent, self-absorbed, beautiful father.

Late that afternoon, Rou's housemaid brought her a note on a silver tray. Rou waited for the maid to leave before she opened the small, heavy envelope.

You will join me for dinner at nine. Zayed

Her upper lip curled as she read the note through, twice. She read the note again, making sure it was indeed his handwriting, and his choice of words.

It wasn't an invitation, it was a command. She *would* join him.

This is what she'd waited for. This is the man she'd missed so terribly these past ten days.

Rou tore the note card in half and threw it away.

She would join her husband, but she wouldn't wait until nine tonight. She'd join him now. This wasn't the homecoming she'd wanted. It wasn't the marriage she'd hoped for. The fragile dream inside her had already died. All that remained was the burning need to salvage her self-respect.

Rou changed into white slacks, an emerald-green sweater with tassels and embroidery and leather flats. She brushed her hair until it shone and then pulled it back into a sleek, low ponytail. Dressed, she added just a hint of makeup, enough for polish, enough for courage, and then she marched toward Zayed's office in the palace, the one area she never went, but it was her destination now.

Rounding the corner of the stairs, Rou ignored the security detail outside Zayed's office. They didn't want her to enter. She wasn't supposed to enter without his permission. They all knew when he'd granted permission, and this wasn't one of the occasions, but this afternoon she didn't care. She'd had it. She was done waiting for a turn, waiting to be seen, waiting to be heard.

Barging into his office, she ignored the startled glances of Zayed's staff as she marched toward his desk. She ignored Zayed's expression—surprise giving way to disapproval. She didn't care if he disapproved. Didn't care if the entire palace knew he disapproved, too. She wasn't of his culture, wasn't accustomed to being treated as second-class or subservient.

"I have meetings in Zurich in two days," she said crisply, "and I'm already packed. I don't need to use your jet as I have a ticket reserved on Sarq Air, but I do need my passport back. I believe you have it for safekeeping."

For a moment no one spoke or moved and then every staff member quickly and silently disappeared, leaving Rou and Zayed alone.

The meeting part was true, she thought, heart pounding like mad, but the having packed part wasn't. She'd said she was packed to make her plans sound fixed, firm, but they weren't set yet; they hinged on Zayed. Everything now revolved around him.

It wasn't a new realization but it still made her sick. She'd fallen in love and lost herself. She'd become her mom.

"You're leaving," he said after the last staff member had walked out.

She drank him in, thinking he was even more handsome if such a thing were possible, his hair a little longer, his jaw a little harder, his eyes a little colder. Just looking at him made her heart hurt and her resolve weaken. But no, she couldn't do this, couldn't become this helpless dependent woman, a woman who couldn't function without a man.

Her father, who had once adored her mother, ended up despising her. Foolish, weak, ridiculous, he'd call her. And then years later after the divorce was finally settled and her mother turned to pills to cope, she'd sit and cry and cry, *I'm foolish, and weak, and ridiculous.*

Men despised ridiculous women. And women despised themselves when they became ridiculous.

Rou could not become ridiculous. She couldn't bear for Zayed to ever despise her. She wouldn't give him the opportunity, either.

Her chin lifted a notch. "I miss my work. I need to return to work."

He leaned back in his chair. "That's fine. We agreed that you would continue to work, and that you'd travel for your work."

He didn't care, she thought. She didn't matter. And pain burst inside her, hot, livid, scorching. He would never care for her. He couldn't, too damaged by guilt and loss. "But I won't be returning," she said quietly, fighting to stay in control. "I have an office, and a home, in San Francisco. It's pointless being here. I'm not needed here and I am needed there. Besides, we agreed the marriage was just temporary, so why drag it out?"

He lifted his hands. "Why, indeed?"

Her heart was breaking and he didn't care. He didn't care at all. "So that's that," she flashed, pain and fury getting the best of her. "That's all I had to do? Pack my bags, book a ticket and go?"

"You're not a prisoner. You were free to leave anytime you wanted."

His lack of expression, his lack of emotion, his lack of everything pierced her, wounding her to the core. She'd given up so much for him and it meant nothing to him. "I see how it is then," she said, voice trembling with rage. "You've met your responsibility. You've done exactly as you were required. Married. Become king. And now you have no more need of me."

"I never said that."

"No, but since marrying me you've scarcely spent a moment in my presence. We've had five nights together out of two weeks. The rest of the time you're absent. You don't even return calls. Do you dislike me so much, King Fehr? Is it that difficult, that uncomfortable to spend time with me?"

"I'm not avoiding you to punish you—"

"So you are avoiding me?"

He took a deep breath as if fighting for patience. "I have work to do. Staff and cabinet members and dignitaries to meet. The country was without a ruler for nearly a month, and there's much that happened, much that needs to be attended to."

"But not your new wife. She's just a woman. An afterthought."

"Now you're being childish."

"Maybe," she said slowly, "but at least I'm honest. At least I can say I need more." Her lips curved into a fragile smile. "At least I can admit I needed you."

She waited for him to speak, waited for him to say something that would make sense of the past couple weeks, weeks where she'd tried so hard to be patient for him, and available for him, and do everything she'd want someone to do for her. But he never thought of her. He didn't have the time or ability to think of her.

Seconds crept by without Zayed speaking. Instead he looked at her, his gaze shuttered, his beautiful hard face impassive, and she realized he was hollow and he wanted to remain so. He liked feeling nothing. He liked being dead. But she didn't. Getting close to Zayed had made her aware that feelings and emotions could be good things. Feelings and emotions could add to your life, not detract.

But not if they weren't returned.

And not if they weren't shared.

"My passport?" she whispered, extending her hand. He reached into his desk, unlocked an inner drawer and retrieved her passport. Although he held it in his hand he made no move to stand up and give it to her. He just held it.

Say something, she mentally willed. *Say something that will help me forgive and forget. Something that will allow me to stay.*

But he said nothing, and after a long minute she walked to the desk, reached out and took the passport from his hand.

"Goodbye, Zayed," she said calmly, meeting his gaze, willing the terrible hurt inside her to be still. "Good luck."

Zayed let her go.

From his chair behind his desk he watched her walk out the door, passport gripped tightly in her hand.

If he felt anything, he refused to acknowledge it, suppressing every emotion with ruthless intent. Better to let her walk away now, he told himself. She didn't belong here. She'd never belonged with him. At least this way she'd be safe.

He'd rather hurt than have her hurt, although he knew she already hurt. He had hurt her, despite his promise to protect her. He'd tried to protect her, though. He'd tried to stay away, minimize his impact on her life, keep her from getting entangled in his world and his problems. But his world was complicated and consuming, and he didn't know how to be the king Sarq needed and the man she needed, and his loyalties were clear. Sarq came first. His family second. And Rou...?

He shook his head, jaw clamped so tight it ached.

Rou was tough, and smart. A scientist with a huge career. She'd be fine. She'd always be fine.

Ten minutes later, he heard an engine motor and then from his window he glimpsed one of the palace Mercedes disappearing down the drive toward the gates surrounding the palace compound.

Regret, hot and bitter, rushed through him.

He would miss her. He had missed her these past ten days. God only knew how close he'd come to falling in love with her.

As it was, he didn't sleep well at night. He'd wanted to pick up the phone every other hour in Isi to call her just to hear her voice. She'd been beautiful when she'd stormed his office earlier. The sun had kissed her cheeks, giving her a golden glow while her hair had new, lighter, brighter highlights. In her emerald-green tunic and white slacks she'd looked fierce and fiery and oh so proud.

And oh so hurt.

Regret squeezed his chest, wrapping his heart in a viselike grip.

His Rou. He hoped she'd be fine. She had to be fine. She wasn't a fragile female. She was a modern woman with a demanding career. She'd forget him in no time. He on the other hand…

Zayed put a hand to his temple where it throbbed. It had pounded for days now. Nothing helped it. Nothing would.

If he weren't Zayed Fehr…

If it weren't for the curse…

She'll be fine, he silently repeated. *You're the one that might not recover.*

CHAPTER THIRTEEN

SHARIF FEHR Found Alive.

Heart pounding, stomach churning, Rou read the *Chicago Tribune* newspaper headlines again.

Eighty Days After Disappearance, King Sharif Fehr Alive.

Her hands shook so badly, and the churning in her stomach became genuine nausea. Rou held her breath a moment, battling the queasy sensation, and tried to read the paper, but her hands were still trembling so much that the paper shook, making it impossible to read two words, much less the entire article.

Jerkily she set the paper on the small Chicago coffee shop table and smoothed it flat.

Sharif alive? Alive. Her hands felt clammy and her mind raced. Was it possible? Could it be possible? If so, it was a miracle. A miracle.

My God, *Jesslyn*. Jesslyn and the children. They must be ecstatic. Over the moon.

And Zayed. Zayed…

Tears filled Rou's eyes and she fiercely wiped them

away, trying to read the small print so she could get the whole story.

Following the devastating crash of the royal Fehr jet, Sharif Fehr, badly burned and injured, was rescued from the wreckage by an itinerant Berber tribe. The tribe of nomads didn't recognize King Fehr, and the king, due to head injuries, didn't know who he was, either. A month ago, Khalid Fehr, the king's youngest brother, heard a rumor about a traveling Berber tribe seeking medicine for an injured man and acted on the lead. It had taken him nearly four weeks to locate the tribe in the Sahara but once he did, he recognized his brother immediately. The family has been reunited in Isi, Sarq, where the king is currently undergoing medical care.

Rou stopped reading, put a hand to her stomach, praying the nausea would subside. She didn't want to throw up, not here, not now.

Don't think about it, she told herself, *it'll pass, it always does, and in the meantime, Sharif is alive, and rescued by his brother no less.*

She reached out to the paper, ran her fingers across the headlines. So if Sharif was alive, what did that mean for Zayed?

But just thinking of Zayed made her chest burn and her throat ache, and she had to swallow very hard to make the lump in her throat go away.

Zayed wasn't her concern. Not anymore. They didn't speak—but when had they?—and they'd had no other communication other than in the beginning, just after she'd left. He opened an account for her in San Francisco and wired in the funds he'd promised—millions. And every month he sent more.

She never touched the account. Never even opened the bank statements that came to her house. She didn't want his money. She didn't want him to fund her research center. She didn't want anything to do with him. He'd done enough. He'd broken her heart.

Four hours later, Rou stood at the podium in the downtown Chicago hotel's conference center giving her speech on the biological and chemical effects of falling in love to one thousand members of the American Association of Marriage and Family Counselors. She was talking to the professional therapists about the powerful chemical cocktail that early love was, and how laboratory research had shown that dopamine's effect on the brain was powerful, and addictive, resulting in cravings, behavior changes, sleep disruption and erratic thought.

She talked about how painful the end of relationships were, especially relationships still in that heady, newly in-love stage when dopamine still flooded the system, resulting in physical and emotional pain.

In her cool, clear, scientific voice, a voice that betrayed none of the anguish she'd gone through in the weeks following her departure from Sarq, she lectured on the painful effects of dopamine withdrawal, a withdrawal process that could last months, but would eventually diminish with time. Exercise and activity could help a client cope a little better, but nothing would completely take away the suffering as the suffering was real.

She theorized that one day scientists would develop a broken-heart pill much like the pills one took for depression, but that was years away.

With her speech concluded, she took questions for twenty minutes and then she was done.

Rou stepped off the stage, away from the bright lights into the darker wings, where she grabbed the first thing she found—a plastic rubbish bin—and threw up.

And again.

My God. How was she going to do this? How was she going to get through? She'd never wanted to marry, never wanted to have kids, and now she was heartbroken, eight weeks pregnant and terrifyingly alone.

She could handle being alone. She couldn't handle being pregnant and alone. God only knew what kind of mother she'd be.

King Zayed Fehr stood in the wings of the stage and watched Rou speak. She'd always been slender but was now downright thin, and unusually pale in her simple black suit, a suit he'd hoped she would have replaced with something more flattering, never mind fashionable. She spoke well, though, he thought. Her voice was strong and clear. She made good eye contact with the audience. She answered every question with perfect confidence.

She was doing fine. He'd been right to let her go. She was a cat. She'd always land on her feet.

He was glad that he'd come to see her speak, glad to witness her continued success. The conference room held a thousand and tonight it was packed. He hadn't been able to buy a last-minute ticket and ended up paying a janitor off to let him in, which was why he stood in the wings in the shadows next to the janitor's trolley of cleaning supplies.

But now she was finished and walking off the stage, walking straight toward him. He stepped farther back into the shadows, not wanting to be seen. The moment she left the stage's bright lights, the moment the dark velvet curtains on the sides concealed her, she lurched at the trolley, grabbed the janitor's plastic waste bin and threw up.

She threw up again, and, falling to her knees, sat hunched over the bin, shoulders shaking, body heaving as tears ran down her face.

Rou was sick. The shock of it propelled him forward.

They were in the back of his chauffeured limo heading to the hospital, and Rou was livid. He wasn't listening to her. He wasn't paying her any attention. But then, when did he? "I'm not sick," she repeated, putting down her window a crack to get some of the night's cold fresh air. Cold air always helped her nausea. Ice did, too.

"You're in denial then—"

"I'm not in denial," she interrupted hoarsely, fingers curling into her palms as she willed her stomach to settle. She couldn't get sick again, and not here in the back of his car. "And I don't need a hospital. There's nothing they can do for me—"

"You don't know that," he practically roared.

And Rou, who'd never heard him use anything but a quiet voice, blinked, stunned by his display of temper, and then because it was all so impossible, laughed.

She didn't laugh hard. It was soft, mirthless, because life was so brutally unfair.

"What's so funny?" He was still angry and his voice had a definite edge to it.

"You. Us. All of this." She leaned gingerly against the car door, trying to stay as still as possible. "The fact that you had to marry the one woman in the world that didn't want you. The one woman who never wanted to marry, or have kids." Her eyes shone, and she swallowed convulsively because the nausea was getting worse, not better and it was just a matter of time before she threw up again. "I'm not sick, Zayed. I'm pregnant."

They ended up at the hospital anyway. Zayed either didn't believe her or needed proof, and the doctor, on hearing Zayed's name, immediately ushered them into a room with an ultrasound.

In the small, curtained examination room, the young doctor moved the wand this way and that, staring at the screen intently. Then he nodded, expression intently focused. "Mmm-hmm," he said, moving the wand again and getting a clearer picture. "Okay. So that's what we're dealing with."

Zayed leaned across the bed, trying to see the dark screen. "What?" he barked, strain written in the hard set of his beautiful features.

The doctor turned the screen toward them so they could see, and he pointed to the image. "Two heartbeats." His finger pointed to one, and then another, and then he looked up at them and smiled. "Twins."

For a moment Rou thought she'd faint, and then she fought for air even as her head spun. Twins? "Not possible," she choked, "not possible."

"They run in my family," Zayed answered flatly, no emotion in his voice. "Jamila and Aman."

"But not possible," Rou repeated hoarsely. One baby was bad enough, but two? Hot tears gathered, stinging her eyes.

The doctor turned off the machine and rolled back on his stool. "Congratulations, you are definitely expecting."

Twenty minutes later, they were back in his car, and Zayed's driver was heading toward Rou's hotel to get her things. Rou wasn't speaking, and although Zayed kept a watchful eye on her, he didn't try to fill the silence, either.

She'd been pregnant for eight weeks, probably had known for a month, and she'd never told him.

Probably never intended to tell him, he realized with a heavy sigh. Not that he blamed her. He hadn't been very supportive of late.

He felt a twinge of conscience. Or ever.

But it'd be different now. She was having his children. His children. Babies. Two.

A boy and a girl…or…?

He pictured Jamila and Aman as little girls and how they'd run through the palace playing hide-and-seek, and he felt another twinge, this time of sorrow. His sisters had been such beautiful girls.

Rou stirred in her corner of the car. She clutched a paper bag in her hand just in case she needed to throw up again—which was likely—since she'd thrown up in the hospital's parking lot.

Zayed watched her profile as the driver ferried them back to her hotel. She stared blindly out the window, her expression completely blank. He saw no emotion in her face and that troubled him most. "Are you all right?" he asked as kindly as possible.

"No."

"What can I do?"

She just shook her head, and then shook it again. "I can't have a baby," she said roughly. "I can't have one, much less two."

"I will help you."

"No."

"*Laeela*, darling—"

"Not your darling. Not your *laeela*. I am nothing."

"Just my wife."

"We are not married."

"We are married, and we will always be married. I will never divorce you. I have taken vows—"

"You and your stupid vows!" she cried, finally turning on him. Tears glimmered in her eyes, and her cheeks were dark with color. "You live in a world of vows and curses, superstition and ghosts, and it's a world I don't fit in, nor do I want to be in. I believe in science. I believe in an objective reality. I believe in cold, hard facts. And the facts say you will never, ever love me, and I will not give my life to a man that can't love me."

She was beyond control, beyond reason, and she jammed her thumb to her chest. "I deserve more, Zayed. I deserve so much more."

And then she was crying, hunched over, face covered with her hands, crying as though her heart would break.

In her plain black suit, with her pale hair in a simple ponytail. Zayed stared at her as if he'd never seen her before.

She loved him.

She didn't say the words. She didn't have to. He saw it in her eyes when she looked at him. Heard it in the anguished tone of her voice. Felt it in the wrenching sobs of her body.

She loved him and he'd hurt her. Badly. So badly.

His chest burned with guilt, but more than that, with sorrow. As she cried in the corner of the car he thought she looked like a girl, not a scientist, and he wondered why he'd never seen the girl before.

He reached out to touch her and she jerked her shoulder away. "Don't."

He started to draw his hand away when he saw her tears slide through her fingers, and fall on her knees.

She was so alone. No family, few close friends. Who would comfort her if he didn't?

Who would love her, if he didn't?

And the realization was like fire in his chest, a fire ripping his heart wide.

She did need him. Not just anyone, but him. And why him, he didn't know, but he remembered from her speech at the podium that love was strange and random and unpredictable, and rare.

Who knew why she loved him, but she did, and it mattered to him, mattered immensely.

Mattered more than anything else he could think of. And Zayed reached for her again and, ignoring her attempt to evade him, lifted her off the seat and onto his lap and held her against his chest as she cried.

"Do not cry, sweet girl," he murmured, stroking her hair and kissing her temple. "Do not cry. I am here and I love you and I will not leave you. Not ever, not again. I promise."

He ended up staying with her that night in her hotel room. She said it was because he didn't trust her not to run away. He said it was because he didn't want to leave her alone, not when she was so sick.

Rou hadn't wanted him to stay, but she didn't have the strength to make him leave. Instead she took a quick shower, pulled on her flannel pj's and then climbed into bed.

In bed, Rou turned away from Zayed so he couldn't see her face. She couldn't bear to look at him, much less to have him look at her.

She was so mad at him. She was so mad and so hurt and so sick.

Heavens, she felt sick. She felt as though she had the flu, a flu that had lasted for weeks on end.

It'd been bad enough knowing she was pregnant, but now, pregnant with twins? Two babies? Two people she could hurt? Two people she'd damage…maybe destroy?

And now Zayed was here. He'd come back. Come back for her. This is what she'd wanted, wasn't it?

This was to have been her moment of vindication. Her whole childhood she'd waited for her father or her mother to realize that they were wrong, and that they loved her and missed her and needed her. They never did, not in their lifetime, but now Zayed was here, and he said he wasn't leaving again, that he'd always be there for her now.

So why wasn't she happy? Why didn't this feel like a victory?

Why was she so sad?

Because he was here out of duty. He was here to fulfill his responsibilities. He was here because he had to be, not because he wanted to.

And Sharif. They hadn't even talked about Sharif yet, but somehow in the last couple of chaotic hours, Sharif's return became less significant than the two little lives growing inside her.

Two lives. Impossible. Improbable. Why had birth control never been part of her mind-set? Why had she not stopped to consider something so basic, so practical, so essential?

But she hadn't, and now everything would forever be different.

Zayed waited until Rou was asleep before joining her in bed. He lay awake long after he lay down. His thoughts turned, his mind working ceaselessly.

Sharif had returned, still injured, but at least alive. Jesslyn and the children were happy beyond measure. Khalid's wife, Olivia, had delivered a healthy baby boy. And now he was going to be a father.

Peace and prosperity had been restored to the palace. Sarq was filled with one celebration after another.

Maybe the curse was weakened.

Or maybe, just maybe, it was close to being broken.

Or maybe, as Rou had once said, there had never been a curse, just Zayed's own guilt that had tortured him for all these years.

Perhaps it was time to deal with the terrible guilt, and his own punitive conscience. Perhaps he could consider other ways to look at life and its challenges. Perhaps he could even consider the possibility of happiness.

He looked at Rou, who in her sleep had turned to him, her body finally relaxed and curled trustingly against his. Watching her sleep, he felt his heart burn, and as he lifted a strand of silver-gold hair from her cheek, his heart burned hotter and brighter, until his entire chest hurt.

Rou, his wife.

Rou, the scientist, the mother of his children.

Rou, his woman. His.

His.

The need for possession was so strong, the need to claim her and not own her, but love her, love her freely, love her fully, love her as he hadn't loved anyone since Nur surged through him.

Zayed had to close his eyes as his entire chest and body heated, alive, livid, hot. All the empty and hollow spaces were filled with the fire, and Zayed feared that maybe he couldn't handle so much feeling.

He ground his teeth against the blistering pain. Closed his eyes to try to keep from making a sound.

He hadn't felt so much in years, not since he'd gotten word of Nur's death, and yet what he felt now wasn't grief or death but something far different, something far more complex.

He felt…life.

He felt alive.

The fire was him coming back to life, battling back to life, battling the darkness and destroying it.

A cool hand pressed to his cheek. "Zayed. Zayed?" Rou's voice whispered urgently in the dark. "What's wrong?"

He couldn't speak, couldn't answer her.

She sat up, leaned over him, her long, cool hair spilling on his shoulder. "Zayed! Zayed, look at me!"

It took a great effort, but he did, and as he opened his eyes and focused on her, he wondered why her beautiful face seemed liquid, and then when she wiped beneath his eyes he realized she was liquid because he was crying.

"Zayed, what is it?" she choked, panicked.

He didn't think he'd ever been in such pain, didn't know if he could endure it much longer. Sweat beaded his brow, breaking in tiny blisters across his skin. "I love you," he said, voice low and hoarse. "I love you and need you. Forgive me, *laeela*, my love, but I need you."

And then abruptly the fire was gone, all the fire that had been burning him, in him. The pain was gone, too. Extinguished. Leaving him quiet but exhausted.

"Are you not well?" she asked, confusion coloring her voice.

"I am well," he answered.

"Do you have a fever?"

He understood her bewilderment. "Because I told you I loved you?"

"Perhaps you caught a bug, or food poisoning—"

He didn't want to laugh, but he couldn't help the deep rumble in his chest. "No, love, there's nothing wrong with me. For the first time in twenty years, there is nothing wrong with me."

Rou leaned over, reached out to the lamp on the bedside table and turned it on. She stared at him, wordlessly.

"The curse," he said. "I think it's gone." He hesitated, listened, waited, then nodded. "It is gone. It's finally gone."

"How?"

"I realized how much I loved you, and realized how love, even my love, is stronger than superstition and darkness. That love is stronger than anything else there is."

Her lips curved uncertainly. "This all happened in the last hour?"

He felt that rumble of a laugh deep in his chest. "It's been happening for a while. Sharif's return. Jesslyn's happiness. Khalid and Olivia's new son. There was happiness everywhere, and life everywhere, and love everywhere and I couldn't find any sign of a curse. Couldn't find any sign of unhappiness but the unhappiness in me."

"And your unhappiness…?"

"Brought me to you."

"In Chicago."

He heard her crisp scientist voice and he couldn't suppress a smile. "Yes, in Chicago. I came to find you."

"Why?"

"Why? Because I love you."

She looked at him with suspicion. And then looked at him with horror. And then jumped up. "Oh no. Not again. I'm going to be sick!"

While Rou huddled in the bathroom next to the toilet, Zayed called room service and ordered a bucket of ice, a bottle of soda water, a bottle of ginger ale, a plate of dry toast, a plate of plain crackers, a platter of sliced melon and a bowl of chilled grapes. Immediately.

Rou was just climbing back into bed when room service arrived with the cart. Zayed took the trays from the cart, sent the attendant away with a tip and carried everything over to the bed himself.

"Oh, Zayed, I couldn't eat if I tried," she said, seeing the covered dishes and putting a reflexive hand to her middle. The very thought of food made her want to gag.

"It's not just any food," he answered, adjusting the covers and then the trays. "Think of it as magic food. Antinausea food. Olivia, my brother's wife, was sick her entire pregnancy and swore by grapes, melon and ginger ale. Let's see if any of it will help you."

He lifted the cover off a bowl, plucked a small green grape from the stem and handed it to her. Tentatively she put it in her mouth, rolled it around to test her gag reflex and then bit into it. It was cold and sweet, a little crunchy but good. She reached for another. And then ate half the cluster, a couple bites of melon, a half slice of toast and then lay back, content.

"Better," she said, smiling for the first time in days. "Yes?"

"Not cured, but definitely better," she answered. She rested against the pillows, eyes closing, and just breathed in and out, content to just be content. It had been a long and difficult two months. "Two babies," she said after a moment.

She heard him exhale and she opened her eyes. He was smiling. Hugely. "I'm sorry for you," he said, not looking all that sorry, "but very happy for me. I'm going to be a father. We're going to be parents."

A heaviness settled in her chest. "I didn't want to be a mom."

"But you never brought up birth control."

"I know." She frowned, brows pulling. "Isn't that strange? I'm so anal about everything, and I never once thought about it. I guess I didn't think I could get pregnant. Guess I didn't think sex would lead to babies."

He looked at her as if he suddenly doubted her sanity. "You hold multiple doctorate degrees, Dr. Tornell."

"Yes." She rubbed at her head. "I know. Troubling."

He leaned on his elbow, studied her. "Maybe you wanted to be pregnant. Secretly."

"No."

"Maybe."

"No. Absolutely not. I wouldn't be a good mom. I wouldn't be a good parent—"

"Or maybe you knew deep down you would be. Maybe you knew that you're nothing like your mother and you'd never abandon your child. It's not who you are."

Rou drew her knees up toward her chin, eyes gritty and burning. "I wish I could say you were right. I love the sound of it. But it's the opposite that's true. I'm exactly like my mom. That's why I left, you know. I left because I'm foolish and weak, and ridiculous. Just like her."

Zayed stared at her for a long moment before rolling onto his back in laughter. He laughed and laughed and then laughed some more. Rou grabbed one of the pillows and hit him with it. "Why are you laughing?" she demanded. "I just told you my deepest, darkest secret, and you start howling like a hyena!"

He rolled back up, and looked at her, a tender smile playing at his lips. "If you're so weak, how did you find the strength to leave me? If you're so foolish, how is it that you survive on your own without any of my financial or emotional support? If you're so ridiculous, why am I so crazy about you?"

She stared at him, aware of so many different emotions rushing through her. Hope, fear, anxiety, excitement. "Are you crazy about me?" she whispered.

He leaned toward her, pushed long, pale hair back from her face. "Absolutely. One hundred percent."

"How do I know?"

"Because I am here. I couldn't stay away from you. I had to come see you, check on you, make sure you were okay."

"And am I okay?"

"You're okay, but you could be better." His gold gaze rested on her face. "You could be with me. We could be together. We could have what we both want…what we both need."

"And what is that, Dr. Fehr?"

His teeth flashed whitely at her joke. "Love, laeela. We could be together and have love."

She stared at him for so long, searching for the man that would abandon her the first chance he got, for the man who was torn between duties, the man haunted by a ghost, but all she could see was Zayed and he was everything she wanted, and everything she needed. "Are you saying all this because you've lost your job?"

He looked confused and then he choked on a smothered laugh. "I didn't lose my job."

"But Sharif…?"

"Isn't well enough to resume leadership anytime soon." The laughter faded from his face and voice. "It's not in the news—we've withheld the information from the media, but Sharif still doesn't have all of his memory back. His head trauma was quite severe and doctors are adamant that he has all the time he needs to rest and recuperate."

Rou sagged back against her pillows. "Does he have amnesia?"

"There is extensive memory loss."

"Does he know Jesslyn? The children?"

"He knows Jesslyn. His memories are of the years he lived in London, before he was king." One of his eyebrows lifted. "He remembers you, though."

But not his own children. Wow. "So you remain king," she said softly.

"I remain king." He leaned toward her, caressed her cheek. "But I can't do it without you. Nor do I want to. I'm lonely. I miss you. You made the palaces happy places for me. They're empty without you. Come home with me. Come be my wife, my queen."

It was tempting, so tempting. She'd been so miserable without him, and being pregnant and alone had made her unhappiness unbearable. But life in Sarq was not necessarily good for her, or healthy. "I don't know, Zayed. I get lost in your palaces. I get lost in your world—"

"You were never lost. Not once. I knew where you were, I knew everything you were doing. You weren't lost. I just hid from you. I was at fault, and I know it. But it won't happen again. I couldn't let it happen. I love you too much to hurt you like that again. I swear, as a man, as a Fehr and as a king. I will not desert you, not emotionally, not physically."

She wanted to believe him. She really did. And yet…and yet… "I want your direct numbers for both palaces," she said, lifting her chin, hoping he couldn't see the tears in her eyes. "A direct line. Even if it means you have to put in a separate line for just me. I don't want to ever go through butlers and valets to reach you. I want to be able to call you when I need you—"

"Your own line. I promise."

"And I want to travel with you. If you're in Isi, I'll go to Isi. If you're in Cala, I'll go to Cala, too."

He smiled, creases fanning from his eyes. "And Monte Carlo? And London? And New York?"

"Yes, yes and yes."

His smile stretched, and he looked more handsome than she'd ever seen him, all dark hair, glowing eyes and beautiful smile. "Anything else, my love?"

Rou thought. She folded her hands in her lap and tried to think if there was anything else, any other conditions, and she realized that the only thing she really needed was time to build trust. But with time, and trust, she knew her fears would fade, and the hurt would heal.

Because she wasn't like her mom. She was strong, far stronger than she knew.

"I want our babies to grow up in a happy home," she said after a moment. "I want us to be strong enough, and loving enough, to always put them first. To put their needs before ours. I couldn't bear it if our children were caught between us. I couldn't bear to have them hurt the way I was."

He leaned toward her, kissed her on the lips. "I agree, completely, wholeheartedly."

She closed her eyes at the brush of his lips. Her lower back tingled and her stomach quivered but with a good quiver for a change instead of bad. She reached to his face, let her fingers trace the magnificent cheekbone and jaw. "I love you."

"I hope so. I need you, and your love. Our babies do, too."

"It will work," she said firmly, decisively. "We can make this work."

"I know we can, too."

Rou smiled and as she smiled at him, Zayed felt his heart trip and his breath catch in his throat.

"Love heals." Rou's voice had softened and she looked at him with bright blue eyes. "It makes everything new." And then she leaned into him, and fitted her lips to his. She kissed him with such tenderness that his heart ached only a moment before feeling joy.

Joy.

He felt joy.

Lifting his hands, he drew them through Rou's hair, letting the long, silken strands fall around them.

His wife, his bride, his joy.

He was a man with many great blessings, but no blessing was greater than this woman, his joy.

EPILOGUE

ROU wanted the babies baptized. It wasn't something the Fehr family usually did, but Jesslyn and Olivia were supportive and Zayed believed that all babies could use blessings, so he agreed to fly in a priest from London.

The service was held in one of the smaller palace reception rooms and the ceremony itself was to be short and sweet—necessary, as the babies, now nearly six months old, wouldn't have tolerated more than that.

Rou had chosen Zayed's brothers as the infant boys' godfathers. She watched now as quiet, serious Kamil was placed gently into his uncle Khalid's arms; and fierce, stubborn infant Sharif, Kamil's identical twin brother, went to Uncle Sharif.

King Sharif smiled as he took the six-month-old infant into his arms, looking down at his namesake and then at Rou. Rou's chest squeezed tight with emotion, and she smiled back at the man who was both friend and brother-in-law, a man who'd worked so hard this past year to recover his memories and regain his physical strength.

Zayed, sensing that Rou was close to tears, slipped an encouraging arm around her waist, but it was too late. She could barely focus on the ceremony, her vision already blurred. It was such a miracle, she thought, Sharif here, once again king, and it had been only natural to name one of the babies after him.

With Sharif back, and resuming his role, she and Zayed were free to go anywhere, but they'd decided to stay in Sarq, and to live and raise the boys in Cala at the summer palace. She loved the water and the weather and the beautiful historic port. Zayed wanted to be close to his family but not tripping over them, so Cala was a perfect solution. Zayed had also said they could start traveling, if that's what she wanted, but Rou didn't want to travel. Didn't feel any need to get back to work. She loved being a mom. Adored her husband. And thoroughly enjoyed her life.

She, who never wanted to marry or have children, had found her bliss. It wasn't the hours at the office, or on the road lecturing. It was here at home. Her bliss was love, marriage and motherhood. Three areas of study she planned to continue as long as she lived.